KITTENS IN THE KITCHEN

"Just a few days," Mandy said. "We can't move them for a few days in case the mother decides to abandon the kittens. Please let her stay where she is!"

"Stay? In my linen basket!" Mr. Williams snorted. "On my best shirts!" He tossed his head. "A load of smelly cats!"

"They're not—" Mandy interrupted, but James stopped her.

Mr. Williams headed straight at Mandy and James to shoo them out of his kitchen. "Go on, you two. Look sharp!"

"Please!" Mandy pleaded. She felt sick at heart.

"No!" Mr. Williams thundered. "They have to go!" He looked down again at Mandy's terrified face. "I'm telling you once and for all. I'm not having them kittens in my kitchen."

Kittens in the Kitchen

Lucy Daniels

Illustrations by Shelagh McNicholas

BARRON'S

All inquiries should be addressed to:
Barron's Educational Series, Inc.
250 Wireless Boulevard
Hauppauge, NY 11788-3917

ISBN 0-8120-9665-7

Library of Congress Catalog Card No. 95-42921

Library of Congress Cataloging-in-Publication Data
Daniels, Lucy.
    Kittens in the kitchen / Lucy Daniels ; illustrations by Shelagh McNicholas.
        p.   cm. — (Animal Ark series ; 1)
    Summary: When the stray cat she has adopted has kittens in her school caretaker's cottage, he gives Mandy just a week to find homes for the four babies.
    ISBN 0-8120-9665-7
    [1. Cats—Fiction.   2. Veterinarians—Fiction.]   I. McNicholas, Shelagh, ill.   II. Title.   III. Series: Daniels, Lucy.   Animal Ark series ; 1.
PZ7.D2193Ki   1996
[Fic]—dc20   95-42921
                                                        CIP
                                                        AC

PRINTED IN THE UNITED STATES OF AMERICA
987654321

To Jenny Oldfield, who loves animals, and
to Peter and Benjamin, the kittens in my kitchen

One

"Mandy, you're very keen on school all of a sudden," Mr. Hope said. He watched her stuff old newspapers into her schoolbag. She flung on her school jacket, flicked a brush through her dark blonde hair and snatched a mouthful of toast. "It's only ten to eight. Are you sure you're okay?"

"Very funny!" Mandy said. "Of course I'm okay. It's just a special day, that's all." She'd fed her rabbits and done her morning chores at Animal Ark. Simon, the nurse, had come in to take over care of the animals and do temperatures and medicines. Now she was free to go.

"School trip?" Mr. Hope took a guess as Mandy unlocked her bicycle padlock and put on her bike helmet. He got no reply. "New boyfriend?"

"Ha, ha!" Mandy said. "No time now, Dad. I'll tell you later." She set off up the driveway, her long legs pedaling like mad. She waved at her mother.

"What's the rush?" Mrs. Hope rolled down her car window.

But Mandy had already sped by, under the wooden sign, "Animal Ark, Veterinary Surgeon." She took one look back at the old stone cottage with its modern vets' extension to the rear, then she pedaled hard again. Her heavy schoolbag dragged across her shoulder.

"She's up to something," Mandy heard Mrs. Hope say. "She's got that determined look on her face."

Mandy knew they wouldn't have a clue what she wanted with the old newspapers. But she ignored them and charged up the lane towards Welford village. She'd keep her mystery until evening, after Mrs. Hope came back from her round of visits to the sick cats, dogs, goats, and hamsters that made up the busy practice of Animal Ark. She gave her mom and dad one last wave before she turned out onto the road. "See you later!" she yelled.

*   *   *

"This is it! This is the big day!" Mandy greeted her friend James Hunter. As usual, his straight brown hair flopped onto his forehead, and his glasses sat halfway down his nose.

"Hi," he said. "Do you realize I've dragged myself out of bed half an hour early to meet up with you outside this rotten post office!" He was breathless from pedaling. "My dad nearly dropped dead with shock!"

"Come on!" Mandy said, ignoring his protests. "Let's go and see!"

Mandy and James cycled out of Welford on the two-mile stretch into Walton. Past all the sleepy cottages and wide-awake farms with their collie dogs at the gate, she never once stopped chattering.

"It's going to be today, I know it!" She had a feeling about these things. James nodded and panted to keep up. "I'm so excited I can hardly wait!" The ground sped by under their wheels. "She's been looking for a warm, dry place, and that's always a sign! Anyway, she refused her food yesterday." James nodded again in agreement. "I did see her on the custodian's porch yesterday after school, behind the stack of logs. She's a very clever cat!"

They pedaled down the final hill. Mandy's short hair blew back in the wind. The new bungalows of

Walton greeted them, spic-and-span. Walton Moor School lay behind these new houses, another new building that backed onto open countryside. Mandy and James rode through the gate into the deserted playground.

Mr. Williams, the custodian, strode through the grounds, setting out parking cones for the garbage truck. It was Thursday, trash collection day. "Morning!" Mandy called, with James running to catch up. But Mr. Williams was a man of few words. He ignored her greeting.

"Shh, now!" Mandy warned James. They'd left their bikes locked up in the shed, and came up behind the custodian's house. "We don't want to disturb her." Carefully they peered over the beech hedge, neatly trimmed by Mr. Williams. They scanned his pink rose bushes and the porch at the back of his house.

"Mandy," James dared to whisper, "does Mr. Williams know about this?" He was cleaning his glasses on his school sweater. "I mean, what will he say if he finds us snooping about on his porch?"

"He won't mind," Mandy whispered back. How could anyone mind about animals? "Mrs. Williams sometimes puts out food. I bet that's why Walton has chosen their porch to have her babies in!" Mandy's face shone with excitement.

"Walton?" James didn't realize the cat had a name. It was small, black and white and rather ordinary. As far as he knew, it was a stray. But then, Mandy had kept details about the cat pretty much to herself up till now.

"I named her after the school," Mandy said. "According to Mrs. Williams, she just turned up on the main doorstep one night, dumped inside a plastic bag with tiny airholes to breathe through. Can you believe it? People can be so cruel!"

Mandy could feel the prick of tears in her eyes even now. "She was only a young cat and someone just dumped her!" She sniffed and tried to pull herself together. "She would've died if I hadn't come along early next morning and gone to the staff room for some milk for her. She was really neglected. I had to build her up." She squared her shoulders. "Anyway, that was six weeks ago. She's the school cat now, only a sort of half stray. So it's up to us to look after her!"

With that, Mandy eased open the back gate into the Williamses' garden. "Walton! Walton!" she coaxed, bending low and looking under the raised porch into the dark space there. James peered up onto the porch itself, behind the stack of logs. No cat.

"Walton!" Mandy called, a bit more loudly.

A black and white shape trotted across the long shadows of the lawn, and over the flower bed; a round, heavy shape, nearly as wide as she was long, with a low belly. James spotted her first. "Mandy, look!" he said.

Mandy breathed a sigh. They'd gotten here in time. "Hello, Walton," she said. "Here's a nice, comfy place for you to give birth to your lovely kittens, see!" She climbed the porch steps. The cat followed. Mandy delved into her bag and pulled out the old newspapers. She showed them to Walton and let her sniff them. "See, nice and warm and dry!"

Then she and James banked up some of the logs to make a sort of den for Walton. They lined it with the newspapers, carefully overlapping them in thick layers. "See!" Mandy said again.

Walton brushed against Mandy's bare legs. She tilted her head up towards the special bed of logs and newspapers. Her delicate nose and whiskers seemed to approve, for she climbed, slow and heavy, up onto the ledge.

"It's in the sun, nice and warm," James said. "Good idea!" He grinned at Mandy, then blushed. In the distance, the morning bell sounded. "Was that the bell?" he asked clumsily. Then he shot off for homeroom before Mandy could reply.

"You hear that, Walton?" Mandy said. "That's the bell. I have to go." But she felt the strong pull that the cat had over her. Perhaps it was because she, Mandy Hope, aged thirteen, of Animal Ark, Welford, Yorkshire, was very like Walton, the school cat. They were both adopted. Her own parents had died in a car crash, too early for her to remember them, and Adam and Emily Hope had taken her in. Now she would do the same for Walton.

Softly she stroked the cat, then she caught hold of herself. "I'll stop fussing now and leave you to cope." She knew animals liked privacy at this time. "No one will bother you, and I'll be back later to see how you've managed." Quietly she backed down from the porch, then quickly she cut across the garden, through the gate and over the asphalt of the playground. The second bell had rung.

Mr. Williams, in his padded green vest, his old corduroy trousers, and his big laced boots, crossed paths with Mandy as she ran into school through the main door. As usual, he only grunted, head down and grumpy. Mandy thought it was best not to say anything to him about Walton and her arrangements for the birth. Leave it till later. Even Mr. Williams's heart would melt once he saw Walton's kittens nestling on his back porch!

Mandy rushed into class. She tried, and failed, to concentrate all the way through math, geography, and English.

At half past three James was waiting for Mandy at the lockers. "Ready?" he asked. Like Mandy, animals were the most important thing in James's life.

Dodging the crowds, they sprinted together up the slope to the custodian's house. Mandy could hardly breathe for excitement. This was Walton's big day!

"Walton!" Mandy called, opening the gate and crossing the lawn. They turned the corner up onto the porch. Mandy half closed her eyes. There Walton would be, tucked up in her newspaper bed, shielding her new kittens! She couldn't wait!

She opened her eyes. The bed was empty! Clean and dry and quite empty. Mandy looked at James. They felt the bottom of the world fall out.

"Where is she?" James gasped.

Mandy shook her head. "It's today. I'm sure it's today." She couldn't understand it. She'd seen enough cats giving birth to kittens at Animal Ark to know just how they looked when the great day came. Mandy and James stood on the porch, confused and alarmed.

"Listen!" Mandy said. The Williamses' back door

stood open in the afternoon sunshine, and Mandy was sure she'd picked up a sound from inside. A tiny, high-pitched squeaking sound!

James stared at her. "What is it?"

Mandy stepped across the kitchen threshold. "Mr. Williams?" she whispered. "Mrs. Williams?"

The kitchen was neat and clean, scrubbed to perfection. Its lace curtains shone pure white. Its black and white tiles looked like an advertisement for floor cleaner. But it was empty. The squeaking noise was slightly louder. "In here!" Mandy said.

They tiptoed into the empty room.

"It's still very muffled," James said. He looked inside cupboards, trying to find the noise.

They looked under shelves, behind the vegetable rack, but still the noise escaped them.

"Walton!" Mandy called gently.

But Walton, wherever she was, didn't want company. Only the muffled, faint squeaking continued. Mandy followed it until she finally tracked it down.

There was a laundry basket in the corner of the kitchen, by the washing machine. It was an old-fashioned straw one with a lid. Mandy put her ear to it. The squeaking came from inside!

Gingerly she lifted the lid. It was dark and warm in

there. The high-pitched noise rose to a wailing chorus. Mandy adjusted her eyes to the darkness and peered inside. She saw the black and white patches of Walton's fur; she saw the cat's eyes glint as she looked up. Obligingly, Walton lifted a paw and shifted sideways. "Look!" she seemed to be saying, "Four perfect kittens!"

Mandy could just make them out—four tiny curled-up things, gray and blind. Skinny, helpless creatures. She thought they were the most beautiful things she'd ever seen!

"Aren't they wonderful!" Mandy breathed, as James came to look over her shoulder.

He saw their blunt little faces and blind eyes. "Ye-es," he said. He clearly needed more time to get used to them.

"Oh, but they are!" Mandy cooed. She touched Walton gently under the chin. "Clever girl!" she said. The kittens squeaked louder in protest at the light and the cooler air. Mandy gave in and replaced the laundry basket lid.

And then their luck ran out. Someone crossed the porch and filled the kitchen doorway. He was tall, bulky, and his feet made a noise across the wooden floor of the porch. "Amy?" he called. He paused, wiped his feet, then stepped into the kitchen.

"Mr. Williams! Um, hello!" Mandy said feebly. James stood alongside her, straightening his school tie, trying to look braver than he felt.

"What the heck!" Williams bellowed with shock. "Amy! Where are you? What the heck!" he said again.

His wife came tottering through from the front room. She was slightly deaf, slightly near-sighted. "Don't shout, Eric," she sighed. "I can hear perfectly well without you having to shout!"

"Oh, can you?" her husband fumed. "I'll bet you heard these two prowling around in here perfectly well, too!"

Mrs. Williams sighed again. "Sit down, all of you," she said. "Everybody sit down while I make us a cup of tea!" It was clearly her cure for everything.

Mandy and James sat down as they were told, as far away from Mr. Williams as possible, while his wife made the tea. "Well!" he said over and over. "Can't a man even call his house his own any more?"

"Oh, shush, Eric!" his wife said, giving him his favorite mug and a butter cookie. "Just give them a chance to explain!' She was little and skinny, half his size, but Mandy and James could see who was boss. "Well, then," Mrs. Williams smiled sweetly

at Mandy. "I'm sure there's a perfectly good explanation!"

"There is," Mandy agreed. She looked wildly at James for help.

"The cat had kittens!" James blurted out.

"In your laundry basket," Mandy finished off.

"What!" Mr. Williams shot to his feet. He backed off into a corner.

"Wait!" Mrs. Williams went to investigate. She lifted the basket lid and peered inside. "It has," she confirmed calmly. "It had kittens, all right."

"On my best shirts!" Mr. Williams stammered. "It had kittens on my best shirts!"

"Calm down, Eric!" Mrs. Williams shook her head. "It's only a stray cat!"

"Only!" The custodian rolled his eyes in helpless anger.

"She won't do any harm," Mandy broke in. "They're very clean animals. She won't leave any mess!" She tried to reason with him. "If you just leave her and the kittens in peace in there for a few days, they'll soon be on their feet. Then you can make them a better place—a cardboard box, for instance. Just line it with newspaper and put it out on the porch. That should be fine!"

"A few days!" Mr. Williams repeated. His face seemed to be stuck. His mouth had dropped open; his eyes were bulging.

Mrs. Williams took Mandy and James aside. She shook her head. "It's no use. He can't stand them."

Mandy was slow to catch on. "Can't stand what?" Only now was she beginning to sense that there was a problem.

"Cats. He can't stand them. They set his nerves on edge."

Mandy breathed in deeply. How could people hate cats?

"He says they dig up his garden. He can't abide

them." Mrs. Williams sounded sorry, but she sounded as if they'd just have to understand. Her husband was stubborn as a mule over cats. She turned and started clearing away the tea things.

"Just a few days!" Mandy said, dashing from one to the other. "We can't move them for a few days in case the mother decides to abandon the kittens. She might, if they get moved. Please let her stay where she is!" She felt breathless with fright, but she tried not to show it.

"Stay? In my laundry basket!" Mr. Williams snorted. "On my best shirts!" He tossed his head. "A load of smelly cats!"

"They're not—" Mandy interrupted, but James stopped her. He had a better idea of when to answer back than Mandy.

"Not likely!" Mr. Williams headed straight at Mandy and James to shoo them out of his kitchen. "Go on, you two. Look sharp! I won't warn you again!"

Mandy and James backed off towards the door. Mr. Williams towered over them. "Please!" Mandy pleaded. She felt sick at heart.

"No!" Mr. Williams thundered. "They've got to go!" He glanced at his wife. "And there's no use you looking like that, Amy, so you can just pipe down!

I'm saying no and I mean no!" He looked down at Mandy's terrified face. "I'm telling you once and for all, I'm not having them kittens in my kitchen!"

Two

Mr. Williams said his final word, then stormed out of the room. Tears sprang to Mandy's eyes. She looked in desperation at Mrs. Williams.

The old woman raised her eyebrows and rolled her eyes. She patted her neat gray hair. "Just give him a minute to cool down," she said. She lifted the laundry basket lid to take a peek for herself. "My, my," she murmured.

"He can't mean it," Mandy said to James, who was trying to drag her out of the kitchen onto the back porch. "He can't just sentence four perfectly harmless kittens to death, can he? It isn't fair!"

James shook his head and kept on pulling. "Come on, we'd better go!"

"Mrs. Williams!" Mandy pleaded.

The custodian's wife carefully washed the rose-patterned teacups. She put them away in a high, glass-fronted cupboard. "I'm saying nothing," she said steadily.

Mandy shook herself free of James. "But it isn't fair, is it? I mean, what have those poor little kittens ever done to anybody? They deserve a chance to live, just like anyone else! You can't just chuck them away because they happen to have been born in an unusual place!"

"On top of my husband's best shirts," Mrs. Williams reminded her. "My Eric's very particular about his shirts." She turned to face Mandy, who was a head and shoulders taller, but thin as a piece of string. "Anyhow, whoever said life was fair?"

"But if he moves them, they'll die! Walton will abandon them!" Again the tears pricked her eyelids.

Mrs. Williams stared up at her. "Walton?" She folded her arms and kept her gaze steady.

"The mother cat. I've called her Walton after the school. I wanted her to sound as if she belonged somewhere! As if she was looked after, and had a home, and somebody who cared!" Mandy rushed on.

The tears were rolling down her cheeks now. They ran with a salty taste into her mouth. She remembered the half-starved cat being dumped in the school doorway. She thought of herself. What would have happened to her if Emily and Adam Hope hadn't taken her in and cared for her when she was tiny?

"Mandy!" James whispered. "Don't cry. You see worse things than this at the Ark every day of the week, remember."

"No, let her alone," Mrs. Williams said thoughtfully. "She's right. They deserve a chance." She took Mandy by the hand and sat her down at the table. Late afternoon sun filtered in through the white net curtains. "But for goodness' sake, dry your eyes, young woman. I can hear my Eric coming back across the yard, and he can't abide waterworks!" She pulled a clean handkerchief out of her apron pocket and handed it to Mandy. "Quick, blow your nose!"

"Will you help us?" Mandy whispered. The custodian's big boots tramped up the steps and across the porch. "If you let the kittens stay, I'll come here every day, twice a day, to help look after them! I'll—"

"Shush!" Mrs. Williams warned. Her husband hung his cap on the door peg. She stood up and leaned forward evenly, with clenched fists down on the table.

"What the — !" Mr. Williams's face darkened as he caught sight of Mandy and James. "I thought I'd told you to clear off! What's the matter; are you deaf?"

"Now, Eric," Mrs. Williams began steadily.

"Don't you 'now, Eric' me!"

"Now, Eric!" she insisted. "This young girl has been explaining to me again about these kittens being moved. It seems the mother won't have any more to do with them if we interfere. They have to be left alone."

A loud meow of agreement from inside the basket backed up the end of Mrs. Williams's firm speech. Thin squeaks followed after in a kind of chorus. Mr. Williams paced up and down the kitchen.

"Stand still, Eric, and listen!" Hands on hips, the tiny woman in the flowery apron confronted her heavyweight husband. "Where's the harm in it? You've a drawer full of shirts up those stairs, most of them hardly worn. There's even one still in its package, pins and all. The one that your sister gave you last Christmas!" She eyed him sternly.

"You know I don't like shirts straight from the wrapping," he grumbled. "They're stiff and they itch!"

"I'll wash it specially." She didn't flinch. "Then you

can wear it this Sunday to church, all right?"

Mandy held her breath. She had the good sense not to interfere in this argument, even though the little wailing sound from inside the basket was tugging at her heartstrings. James still stood sentry by the door, ready to escape.

Mr. Williams pointed an accusing finger at the basket. "My best blue shirt! My favorite!" he reminded her angrily. But it was the last trace of resistance. He knew when he was beaten.

"Now, Eric, it won't come to any harm. This young girl knows all about animals, don't you?"

Mandy nodded and gasped. "My mom and dad are both vets. In Welford, at Animal Ark!"

Mrs. Williams nodded too. "See, she's a good girl. She's promising to come in here twice a day to help look after those poor wee things. They won't get under your feet. They'll just stay in there nice and cozy while Walton tends them."

"Walton?" Mr. Williams interrupted, looking curiously at Mandy.

"The mother cat," Mrs. Williams said, steady as ever.

"Crazy name for a cat," he grumbled, but he was definitely weakening.

"Well?" the fierce little woman demanded.

"Well . . ." He scratched his lined forehead with broad, work-worn fingers.

"Right, that's settled then!" she said, like a suitcase snapping shut. "The girl will come in here each day until the kittens can begin to fend for themselves."

Mr. Williams grunted.

"That means yes," she reported to Mandy and James.

Mandy jumped up from the table, able to breathe at last. "Oh, thank you!" she said in a rush. "I'll go right away and get some food and extra vitamins and things for Walton. I'll be back as soon as I can. Walton will need lots of looking after, being such a small cat, and we may have to help her feed her kittens. I'll bring milk and a dropper just in case. She won't have that much milk herself, and four is a lot for her to feed, especially being so run down when she was a stray! We'll need to—"

"Whoa, hold your horses!" Mr. Williams backed off against the wall. "Not so fast." He turned to James. "Now listen, lad, maybe I can talk sense to you!"

James stood at attention, ready to listen.

"Man to man, I'm telling you straight. My wife Amy is too soft-hearted by far. Everyone knows that. And I've agreed to let those darn kittens stay put on top of my shirts because of her. I don't like it, but I want a quiet life. And when my wife makes up her mind about something, I generally give in."

Mrs. Williams smiled at Mandy, her hands clasped meekly in front of her.

"But," said Mr. Williams, "I just want to give your girlfriend here a word of warning."

Mandy saw James's face turn red at the word "girlfriend." But Mr. Williams thundered on.

"Now, I'm a mild-mannered chap, but before you both go running off for food and vitamins and whatever else, I want to make it clear that I won't put up with these smelly things camping out on my best shirts for a day longer than necessary, is that clear?"

James nodded. Mandy moved over to the door to stand beside him. They watched Mr. Williams's face take on the old angry look. "Quiet life or not, I'll give you just one week," he warned. "And that'll be that! After that, it's the end for the nasty little creatures!"

Mandy felt her heart go thump. She felt the blood drain from her face. "What do you mean?"

"I mean what I say. I'm giving you seven days. Find good homes for those kittens within the week, or else!" He stood with his feet planted wide apart, his face like a storm.

"Or else what?" Mandy gasped.

"Or else I'll deal with them myself!" He turned and stamped out of the kitchen, slamming the door after him.

James and Mandy flew back home on their bikes, up and down the hills to Welford. At the back of her mind hammered the horrible phrase, "deal with them myself." Meaning what? Pictures of kittens drowning, hanging, being dumped in a sack by the side of a highway flashed through her head.

She yelled goodbye to James at the Fox and Goose crossroads and hurried on up the track to Animal Ark. When she arrived, she threw down her bike in the backyard and rushed straight into the office.

"Mom!" she called. She dashed past Jean Knox in Reception, who was busy signing out Miss Martin's Yorkshire terrier, Snap.

Jean looked up and smiled. "She's in the exam room," she said, but the door was already swinging shut.

"Mom!" Mandy slowed herself down and lowered her voice so as not to disturb the animals in their rows of cages and kennels.

"Hi, Mandy, over here!" Mrs. Hope called. She had a blue-gray Persian cat up on the treatment table and was carefully feeling behind his left ear. She gave the cat a kindly stroke and popped him back in his carrier. "You're just about ready for home," she promised. She turned to Mandy. "Now, what's all the drama?"

Her mom stood there in her white coat. She wore her long red hair tied back as usual, but it was always escaping. With her big green eyes and friendly face, Mrs. Hope had the knack of calming Mandy down. "The school cat had four kittens," she reported.

"Ah!" Mrs. Hope smiled. "That explains the newspapers. Good bedding for a birth. Did you get there on time?"

"Yes, but she didn't like the place on the porch that we'd fixed up for her." Mandy fiddled with the catch on the Persian's basket.

"No. They often don't." Mrs. Hope hooked her thumbs in her coat pockets. "So?"

"So she gave birth in the custodian's kitchen instead."

"And?"

"And Mr. Williams, the custodian, hates cats!" Mandy looked at her mother with her wide blue eyes.

"Ah!' Mrs. Hope settled back against the treatment table. Mr. Hope came out of one of the treatment rooms to join them.

"Mo-om!" Mandy began to plead. "He's given us a

week. We have to find homes for four kittens in a week. Otherwise he's threatening to take them off somewhere and put them down!"

Mrs. Hope looked at her husband. "Hmm."

"It's not fair!" Mandy exploded. "He cares more about his stupid shirts than about the lives of four innocent animals! How can anyone be so mean?"

"Calm down, Mandy," Mr. Hope said. He was rubbing his beard thoughtfully. "What's this about shirts?"

Mandy explained. "Anyway, the kittens will be up and about in a few days, then it'll be okay to move them out of the stupid basket. Then he can have his rotten shirts back!"

"Mandy!" her mom warned. "Don't be rude. Some people just don't like cats, and you have to accept that." She lifted the cat basket and began to head for Reception.

Mandy realized that her chance was slipping by. "Mom," she said, "can I take some milk and some vitamins back over there tonight?" She knew from watching her parents at work in Animal Ark what help Walton would need to feed the kittens.

"Of course," Mrs. Hope nodded. She was already on her way out.

"And, Dad, can we take the kittens in here at the

end of the week? Please!" Mandy sidled up to him.

"Ah!" Mr. Hope put an arm around her shoulder. He knew Mrs. Hope was still listening. "Now, Mandy, you know our rules about that."

"I know, Dad, but this is different!" Mr. Williams was going to kill the poor little things if she couldn't find them homes!

"We don't take in strays, you know that. We're not a charity, remember. We're vets." Mandy guessed that it was a rule he might have bent a little. But his wife had a very firm business head. She came back towards them.

"The answer's got to be no, Mandy." Mrs. Hope was kind but firm. She put the cat basket down and spoke gently. "Listen, the custodian has already done you a favor and given you a week, hasn't he?"

Mandy hung her head and nodded miserably. "It would only be for a while, Mom. We'd only have to have them for a while until Walton's finished feeding."

"Then what, hmm?" Mrs. Hope glanced at her husband to check. "That's right, isn't it, Adam? We can't suddenly change our rule about strays. We'd be overrun with them in no time. You've got to understand that, Mandy."

Mandy nodded again. Her mom was always right,

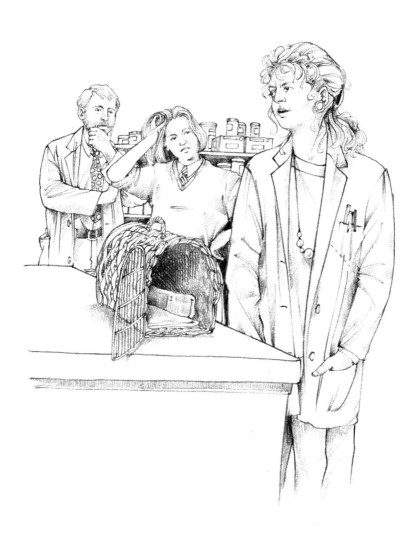

but it hurt a lot to agree with her sometimes. She thought of the four helpless kittens being carefully licked clean by a proud Walton.

"Now, listen," Mr. Hope said in his cheerful voice. "Cheer up, this is a challenge!"

Mandy sniffed and looked up. "How do you mean?"

"You've got a whole week; look at it that way! One week to find four good homes for four furry bundles of fun. You can do it!"

She looked up at his lopsided, cheerful grin. "I can," she agreed. "Or rather, *we* can!"

"We?" her mom asked.

"Me and James."

"You and James!" her mom echoed, raising her eyebrows. "Well, then!"

Mandy ignored her. "Yes! Four homes for four kittens!" Mandy began packing sterilized droppers and vitamin drops into her pockets. "Easy. No problem!"

"Good girl," Mrs. Hope said, satisfied.

Mr. Hope winked at his daughter. "That's my girl!"

Mandy was dashing about, back to normal. "I'll sort this out, just you wait!" She was out through Reception, grinning at Jean, stroking two black Labradors and a hamster, jumping on her bike and pedaling up the driveway before her parents had time to draw a breath.

Back at school, Mrs. Williams opened the kitchen door to her and watched as Mandy gently lifted the lid of the laundry basket.

"Hello, Walton," Mandy coaxed. Inside the basket it was warm and dark. The cat purred up at her. "Come on, come and have some food!" She picked up the warm, soft cat and cradled her. The four kittens wailed miserably. "Sorry, but mother cats need looking after too!" Mandy said as she closed the lid.

"There!" Mandy said as she set out milk and food on the kitchen floor for Walton. The cat arched her black and white back and rubbed against Mandy's legs. Then she settled quickly and daintily to her supper.

"Come and look!" Mandy whispered to Mrs. Williams. "Walton won't mind." Walton raised her head briefly as Mandy lifted the basket lid once more, then kept on lapping milk. They peered together into the dark nest. Clean and dry, the four kittens nestled on Mr. Williams's best blue shirt—blind and helpless, but quiet now—and snuggled against one another.

"Oh, my!" Mrs. Williams shook her head. "They look like drowned rats!"

"No, they don't. They're beautiful!" Mandy whispered. "Look!"

"Well, at any rate they all look the same to me, all gray and furry and curled up like that."

"No, they don't. They're very different; can't you see?" And Mandy promptly decided to give them names. She picked them up, one at a time. "This one's Smoky, and this one's Patch." She looked carefully at the two remaining kittens, then grinned. "And this one's Amy. And this one's Eric!"

"Oh!" Mrs. Williams stood back, slightly shocked, then pleased in spite of herself. "Are you sure? I mean, I don't know what my husband will say!" She tut-tutted and smoothed her apron.

Mandy smiled and stood up as Walton finished her meal.

The cat leaped up into the basket, back on duty. She sprang down into the dark well, ready to let the kittens suckle. "I think we'll let her manage for now." She put the lid back on, testing it to make sure the cat could push it off easily by herself. "Maybe tomorrow we'll start giving the kittens extra."

"Hmm." Mrs. Williams nodded. "What time will you be back in the morning, then?"

"About eight o'clock. Before school starts."

The custodian's wife showed her out. "Mind you don't forget!"

"No way!" Mandy waved, picked up her bike and set off for home.

The sun was setting over the field as she rode up out of Walton, past the new bungalows out onto the open road. The sky was pure red, the horizon dark brown. Mandy felt the wind. She was pleased with the day, happy that Walton had had such a good birth. She'd be a wonderful mother, even though she was so young herself.

Then Mandy's heart jolted. Smoky and Patch, Amy and Eric were all snuggled up for the night. There was a new world waiting outside for them, a big and dangerous place. Just now they were asleep. But Mandy tensed against the handlebars as she took the final curve down the hill into Welford. Her face frowned. She had a week to find four homes. Mr. Williams's threat lurched out of the lengthening shadows like a giant from a fairy tale. "Find good homes for them kittens within the week. Or else I'll deal with them myself!" he roared. Mandy knew he wouldn't relent. He meant what he said. A death sentence hung over the poor little kittens, and only she could save them!

Three

Mr. Hope glanced up from the television as Mandy wandered in. The living room was low, with wooden beams, a big stone fireplace, and cozy red-patterned carpets on the old stone floor. It was a cold evening, and a log fire crackled. "Got any homework?" he asked.

"I've already done it." Mandy flicked through a magazine. She was frowning and restless.

Mr. Hope looked at her again. "Why not take that back to your gran's?" he suggested.

Mandy nodded. She was thinking, thinking; what to do to find homes for those kittens? But she picked up the little magazine and drifted off down the hallway.

"Where are you off to?" her mom asked as she came in through the front door. She'd just gotten back from her yoga class, relaxed and smiling as usual.

"I have to clean out the rabbit hutch, then I'm off to Gran and Grandad's," Mandy said absent-mindedly. She waved the magazine, still deep in thought.

"Say hello from me!" Mrs. Hope shouted, but she got no answer.

Mandy let Flopsy, Mopsy, and Cottontail out into the run in the backyard while she cleaned out their hutch and laid down fresh straw. Satisfied that their water was clean and that they were safely bedded down for the night, she set off up the lane to her grandparents' cottage.

In the cool evening light the mass of white lilacs in her grandad's garden gave off a strong, sweet scent. Even at this late hour he would be out in his greenhouse, puttering. "Hi, Grandad!" she said with a wave. She stood to wait for him by the new camper van sitting proudly in their side driveway.

"Hello, love!" His face lit up and he came out to greet her. He slid the greenhouse door closed. "Come in, come in. Your grandma's inside writing letters."

He showed her in through the kitchen into the cozy back room. The lamps cast a yellow glow and the flowered curtains were closed. "Hello!" Mandy's grandmother shone her a wide smile. "Guess what I'm doing."

Mandy sat down opposite her at the table. "Writing a letter!" She loved visiting her grandparents. Even when she felt down, like now, somehow they cheered her up.

"Not just any old letter!" her grandmother announced. "This one is special. This one is to the prime minister!"

"Oh!" Mandy tried not to sound too surprised. She was used to her gran knitting impossible cardigan patterns and making gallons of rhubarb and ginger jam, not writing letters to prime ministers. "What is it about?" she asked.

"It's about our post office. There are nasty rumors in the village that they want to close it down. Mr. McFarlane told me about it when I went in to pick up some stamps earlier today."

"Why do they want to close it?" Mandy couldn't imagine life in Welford without McFarlane's post office and shop. She'd bought sherbet in there ever since she was tiny; she'd bought water pistols, bubble gum, comics, and sometimes soap for her mom when they ran out. When she'd forgotten James's birthday last month, she'd popped down to McFarlane's for a flowered card with a terrible verse:

> Here's a birthday treat
> For someone very sweet.
> Kind thoughts and wishes too
> For a friend as nice as you!

Gran raised her glasses onto her forehead. "They say it's too expensive to run. Too expensive, I ask you! Honestly, they don't know what they're talking about! We have to stop them!"

"So Dorothy's writing to the prime minister. Always go to the top is what I say," Mandy's grandad said. "On her best notepaper, of course!" He winked and handed her a glass of homemade lemonade.

"On my official notepaper. I'm writing as chairperson of Welford Women's Institute!"

Mandy looked impressed. Even the prime minister would have to listen to her grandmother when she was on her high horse. "They won't close the post office," she said. "Not after they've read your letter!"

They all chuckled. "You've spoiled my concentration," her grandmother said. She put pen and paper aside. She looked at Mandy's fidgety hands. "Anyway, you have something on your mind, I can tell."

Mandy didn't need a second invitation. The story of Walton and her kittens poured out—how she was the school cat, but Mandy felt she must take charge. How Mr. Williams had no heart at all. How she, Mandy, had to find homes for the kittens. Her grandparents nodded, tut-tutted, and nodded in all the right places. Mandy paused at the critical point and took a deep breath. "Gran," she said, trying to sound very reasonable, "I've been thinking."

"Yes?" Her grandmother gave her a sideways look.

"Well, I've been thinking that a cat would be the perfect thing for you here in the cottage. I mean, it's a bit lonely this far up the lane and you hardly see any neighbors, and a cat is really good company for . . ." She faltered and blushed.

"For old people?" Her grandad finished the sentence. He grinned. He was sixty-five—a gardener, a walker, a cyclist. He was fit as a fiddle.

"Yes," she admitted. "Anyway, they're sweet clean animals, and you don't have to fuss over them. They look after themselves, and—"

"Whoa!" her grandad said. "Hold on!" He looked helplessly at his wife.

"Look, love," her grandmother spoke gently. "It's a

good idea, and it's very good of you to be thinking of us like this, it really is. You're our beautiful, warm-hearted girl, you know that!"

Mandy saw a great big "But" looming on the horizon. "Yes?" she said, feeling her heart sink.

Her grandad took over. "But we've just bought our smart new van. You know, our retirement treat!" He jerked his head sideways. "There she stands in the driveway all shiny and new, waiting to take us to the Italian Alps, to Provence, to Portugal!"

"To Scarborough, the day after tomorrow!" her grandmother put in.

Mandy nodded. "So?"

"So we won't be at home to look after a pet as much as we were when your grandad was working. We'll be out on the open road, the freeway, with the wind in our hair and the sun on our faces!"

Mandy was shocked. She wondered if she'd ever see her grandparents again!

"Not all the time," her grandad corrected. "I still need to keep an eye on my tomatoes!"

"But too much of the time to be able to take in one of your stray kittens," her grandmother said finally.

And Mandy had to accept that. Smoky was the one she'd been planning for them to have, with his cheeky face and his way of pushing the other three kittens out of the way when they were feeding. Now Smoky wouldn't be sunning himself on her grandad's patio after all. Mandy tried to swallow her disappointment.

"But . . ." her grandmother said, sweeping stray hair up into the bun at the back of her head, "we can still help!"

"How?" Mandy leaped at the promise. Her eyes lit up.

"We'll help you look for homes. How many kittens are there? Four?" Gran got on her thinking cap. "There's Eileen Davy at the Old School House, but she's on the main road, and she's already lost two cats to the traffic, poor things. There's Myra Hugill, but she has to look after her sick sister in York at present. There's Dora Janeki from Syke Farm, but she's a loony old thing and her new husband isn't known as an animal lover!"

Mandy seized each name, then let it drop as her grandmother counted them off on her fingers. She was beginning to feel hopeless again.

"Wait!" her grandad said. "I've just had a brilliant idea!"

Mandy swung around to face him. "What?"

"The post office!" he said, raising a finger.

Mandy looked puzzled. "Not the post office just

now, Grandad. We're talking about Walton's kittens!"

"I know. That's why I mentioned McFarlane's. That's my brilliant idea!"

"Oh, I see!" her grandmother said. "Yes, Tom, of course!"

"What? What?" Mandy didn't see at all.

"The bulletin board in the post office! That's what we need!" Her grandad took a postcard out of the bureau and uncapped his old fountain pen. "Watch."

He wrote in beautiful old-fashioned letters:

WANTED!
FOUR GOOD HOMES
Cat lovers needed to provide
homes for kittens.
Please call Welford 703267

"There!" he said, standing back and looking at his work of art. "You can take it down to McFarlane's first thing in the morning!"

Mandy took the card. She nodded and smiled "Brilliant, Grandad!"

He screwed the top back on his pen. "It's nothing, my dear," he said modestly.

"Yes, it is, it's brilliant! We'll get millions of calls, you'll see!" Welford was full of animal lovers, and this was the perfect way to find them. Everyone went into the post office at some time during each day. Mandy hugged both her grandparents.

"Maybe not millions," her grandmother advised.

"All right, dozens!" Mandy said, laughing at her own habit of exaggerating. They all laughed together.

She left the house, smiling and happy. She closed the gate with its Lilac Cottage sign, waved and set off down the lane. Tomorrow was Friday. She'd be down at McFarlane's with the dawn, before the paperboy or the milk delivery. She'd spend the weekend coping with all the phone calls. She ran home full of plans and preparations.

Mandy had arranged to meet James again to go into school early. She'd already been into the post office and pinned up her "Wanted" card right in the center of McFarlane's board. She greeted him cheerfully with, "You're seven minutes late, James Hunter!"

James pushed his glasses back onto the bridge of his nose. "Sorry," he said. He screeched to a halt on his bike. "I had to walk Blackie. Dad's away. And then I had to feed Benji."

"Oh, well, then," Mandy forgave him. Being late because of a dog and a cat was quite understandable. "Let's go!"

They made up some time on the journey. Traffic was still light and they knew all the back ways. By five past eight they were knocking on the Williamses' kitchen door.

Mrs. Williams opened it with a worried face. "I thought you weren't coming! Come in, come in," she said.

"Is something wrong?" Mandy was unpacking cat food and a carton of milk on the kitchen table.

"I'm not sure. It's too quiet in there for my liking. Not like yesterday with all the racket. Even Eric noticed." Mrs. Williams watched anxiously.

Mandy lifted the basket lid. "Hello, Walton!" she said. But the cat lay on her side and only managed a feeble meow. "Leave me in peace," she seemed to say. She raised her head, but she didn't stretch and make her way out into the daylight to get some breakfast.

"Poor thing, she's exhausted!" Mandy said. "James, you'd better open that can of food. I'll lift her out." She reached in, tenderly lifting the tired cat. "She'll be all right in a minute," she told Mrs. Williams. She knew from helping out at home that there was nothing seriously wrong. "She just needs looking after." And she set her down to feed.

Walton wobbled, steadied and settled eagerly to the dish of meat.

"What about the kittens?" James said.

Mandy cast an expert eye over the four huddled shapes. "Fine!" she said. "But we'll have to feed them. We'll need the droppers. And we'll have to use the ordinary milk for now." She'd seen her mom and dad do it often enough. Now she hoped she could manage it all by herself.

James got the droppers from her bag. Mandy gently heated the milk. Then she lifted one of the feather-light bundles. She sat with it on her lap and eased open its tiny mouth. "Come on, Patch, come on!" she coaxed.

She squeezed the rubber bulb of the dropper and took in milk from the warm pan. Then, while she held open the kitten's mouth with two fingers, she eased the glass tube between its lips with the other hand. She squeezed again and watched Patch's tiny tongue lick and then swallow the liquid. "See?" she said to James. "Now you have a try."

He nodded and took another kitten, Smoky, out of the basket. Afraid but determined, he copied Mandy's actions with a second dropper. Smoky looked surprised, then gulped. James looked up in triumph.

"Well done!" Mandy said.

It was fifteen minutes later and they were just finishing with the last two kittens when Mr. Williams tramped back in from unlocking the school. James and Mandy were busy stroking the kittens' throats to encourage them to swallow. Mr. Williams heard the tiny mewing from the basket. "What's up with the mother cat, then?" he barked.

"Tired out," Mrs. Williams said. "And you would be, too." She hovered by the sink like a worried relative.

"Hmm." He turned back out of his kitchen, grumbling.

"This place is being turned into a cat hospital! A man can't even call his home his own any more!"

Mandy and James finished the feeding and cleaned up the room to perfection. Walton was sitting on the step, taking the morning sun. She gave herself a thorough licking. Mandy bent to stroke her. "Good girl," she said. She was relieved when Walton decided it was time to return to her kittens. They watched her walk across the shiny tiles, jump up and nimbly lift the basket lid with one paw. Then she disappeared from sight.

"Clever thing!" James said. He looked at his watch. "It's a quarter to nine," he reminded Mandy.

They said a hurried goodbye to Mrs. Williams and ran out through the garden and across the playground. A strong wind blew white blossom petals diagonally across the pavement. "What do you think?" James asked, pausing before they passed under the great stone arch of the main entrance.

"Oh, Walton will be all right," Mandy said. "She'll just have to take things easy." She hitched her schoolbag higher onto her shoulder and brushed cat hairs off her navy blue skirt. "But I'm not so sure about the kittens now."

Mandy didn't want to scare James, but she thought the cat's milk might dry up. This sometimes happened when the mother wasn't strong. If so, the tiny things would soon starve to death. "We'll have to wait and see. Perhaps Walton will be able to go on feeding them herself."

"What if she can't?" James wanted to know.

Mandy thought of the kittens with their gradually opening eyes, their fluffier coats, their attempts to struggle up onto all fours. They still tumbled and collapsed like rag dolls. She could hold them easily in the palm of her hand. "Well, we'll just have to carry on feeding them ourselves," she said.

All morning long Mandy had kitten worries on her mind. There was the old one of finding four good homes in less than a week, and the new one that she wouldn't confess even to James. But the question kept crowding in on her. It wouldn't go away. Walton was exhausted from the birth. The kittens were clinging to life by a thread. And the question still whirled in her head as Mandy sat and ate her packed lunch in B Hall with Kate and Melanie: Would they need to find homes for the kittens after all? Would the poor little things even survive?

Four

Mandy decided that the best answer to her question was a great big "yes!"

You have to think "yes" all the time, or life will get you down, she told herself. She and James would hand-rear the kittens if necessary. So she set about finding homes for them with even more energy than before.

She and James fed Walton and the little gang of kittens right after school, then they cycled back to Animal Ark. "We're going to make more notices!" Mandy announced. She led James upstairs and rummaged under her bed, looking for some neon pink poster board she'd stored there before

Christmas. "Then we'll be sure that every single person in Welford will read one!"

She liked to work in her room; it was an art gallery of animal posters. Horses and rabbits, dogs and cats stared down from her walls. Hardly an inch of wallpaper showed through, just how Mandy liked it. Mandy and James knelt on the floor to cut small rectangles of pink cardboard. They chose broad black felt-tips and began designing their own ads. "Where will we stick these?" James wanted to know.

"Shh, I'm thinking!" Mandy said. She wanted eye-catching words to draw people's attention. Finally she wrote in big capital letters:

KITTENS IN THE KITCHEN
Bring love into your life.
Cats make cozy companions.
Adopt a kitten. Call Welford 703267.

It was catchier than her grandad's notice. She was pleased as she knelt back to judge the effect, while James finished his much more practical card:

HOMES NEEDED FOR FOUR KITTENS!
Remember, pets are for life!
If interested, call Welford 703267

* * *

"I could put this one on your board in Reception," he suggested.

Mandy nodded. "Good idea. Let's go down and ask Jean before she finishes for the day." She knew Jean liked to know exactly what went up on the bulletin board in Reception.

They went downstairs and through into Animal Ark. Jean had closed the appointment book and was searching for her car keys. She had been their receptionist for five years and she was always losing her keys. Mandy knew all the places they were likely to be. She began helping Jean search.

"Here they are!" Mandy lifted the blue book and handed the keys to Jean.

"Oh, silly me!" Jean said, as she always did. She wore her glasses on a silver chain around her neck and still managed to forget where she'd put them.

James tried not to smile. "Can we put a 'Homes Wanted' notice on your board, please?" he said.

Jean took the card, looked for her glasses, found them hanging down around her neck, and read the words. "That looks fine. Just find a space over there beside all the others," she said.

"Others?" James looked at Mandy. They scrambled across to the board. In the bottom corner there were at least six other "Homes Wanted" cards. James and Mandy's faces fell a little.

"Only three of them are for kittens," James said. Two others were for puppies, one for a pony.

Mandy counted up quickly. "Yes, but that's fourteen kittens needing homes altogether!" Fourteen kittens in a tiny place the size of Welford.

"Come on, chop-chop!" Jean said. She was busy locking cupboards, windows, drawers, and anything else that stood still. "I want to shut up shop!"

They looked again at the notices, trying not to feel downhearted. "Ours is the brightest card!" James said. "And it's in the best position!"

Mandy agreed. "I've had another idea!"

With the second bright pink card in her hand they shot off ahead of Jean, up the driveway and down into the village. "It's Friday. Gran will be playing badminton!" They cycled on past the post office, towards the village hall.

"So?" James overtook Mandy. His football training was coming in handy for stamina. They made for the hall, which was set back from the road, next to the church.

"They have a Women's Institute bulletin board in the entrance," Mandy reminded him.

"Right." James nodded and kept up the pace. Lots

of kind-hearted ladies came to the village hall to do flower arranging and cake icing, besides the Friday evening badminton club. It was a great position for one of their cards.

They almost bumped into Miss Davy from the Old School House as she came out of the hall, racket in hand and not a silver-blue hair out of place. She turned and called in a shrill voice, "Dorothy, one granddaughter!" She smiled at them and continued on her way.

Gran emerged, red-faced and breathless. She wore a bright turquoise track suit. "Mandy!" She gave her a quick peck on the cheek. "How nice. But it's thirteen-eleven, final game. I can only spare a second!"

"Sorry, Gran." Mandy held up her KITTENS IN THE KITCHEN card. "Can we pin this on the bulletin board?"

Mrs. Hope squinted at it. "Oh, the kittens? Yes, yes, of course. Good idea. 'Bye, love!" And she dashed back to finish her game.

Mandy opened the glass door of the bulletin board and made space between lists of flower arrangers for the church, Brownie parades, and a charity drive. She pinned her notice firmly in the center, closed the door, stood back, and admired it.

"Better!" James said.

They were pleased with the evening's work as they finally said goodbye and headed home.

After supper Mr. Hope took Mandy into Animal Ark with a secret smile on his face. "Come and see a new admission," he invited.

Near the door of the residential unit was one of the see-through cages, shaped like a cat carrier but made of clear plastic. Mr. Hope picked it up.

"What is it?" Mandy could see the usual newspaper nest and a roll of soft gray rag, but she couldn't spot any animal in there.

"Squirrel!" Mr. Hope said. A small black nose peeped out of the newspapers. "A baby. Five weeks old." Two large black eyes appeared, and out it came, the size of a hamster, with a long, long tail. Mr. Hope unlatched the cage door and lifted it out. He handed the little gray squirrel to Mandy.

"Oh!" she said. She was speechless with delight. She felt its sharp little feet. She stroked its soft gray back while the baby tried to suck the end of her finger. "Where's its mother?" she asked.

"She got run over."

Mandy gasped, and her face crumpled.

"Yes, I know," he said, looking at her. "And this

little one would have died if someone hadn't found him."

Mandy shook her head. Life could be so cruel.

"You'll never guess who brought him in."

"Who?"

"Old Ernie Bell from the cottages behind the Fox and Goose."

Mandy looked surprised. She knew Ernie Bell as a grumpy, silent old man who shuffled down the village street with his bag of groceries.

"He came in and handed him over. ' 'Ere, veterinary,' he says to poor Jean, 'just check 'im over while I fix up a run for 'im in my backyard. I'll be back for 'im in twenty-four hours. Just check 'e's all right!' And he leaves the little chap with Jean and stomps off to build a wire netting run. Who'd have believed it?" Ernie didn't have the reputation of being soft on animals. Mr. Hope put the baby back in its cage.

"What's the roll of cloth for, Dad?" Mandy bent down to study the squirrel in his cage.

"For comfort; something for him to snuggle up to. Animals need a mother substitute, you know. Something to take the dead mother's place." His voice was warm. He put an arm around Mandy.

"What are you feeding him with?"

"This stuff. It's the bottle food we give to orphan kittens. Why?"

Mandy was making new plans for Walton's brood. She took the box of white powder and read the list of contents and instructions printed on the side. "Can I buy some of this from this week's pocket money?" she asked.

"For your school kittens?" Mr. Hope lifted three boxes down from the shelf. "Go on, take them. You don't have to pay!"

Mandy smiled. "Walton's a bit weak at the moment. We'll have to help her feed the kittens properly."

"Well, this stuff is much better than cows' milk," Mr. Hope said, adding an extra box. "Mix it with boiled water, and use these little bottles with rubber nipples. The kittens can suck these properly. Everything's sterilized, of course."

"How often?" Mandy realized that there was a proper way to do this. The kittens' lives depended on it.

"Every couple of hours for the first week."

Mandy gulped.

"Less if the mother cat can still give milk herself, during the night for instance."

"I think she can. She's just a very small cat, and

she's tired." Mandy was still determined to think the best.

"Well, then, this stuff four times a day will do the trick. Breakfast, lunch, tea, supper." He glanced at Mandy's serious face. "You're going to be busy," he said. "Any luck with finding homes for them yet?"

"Not yet." She bent thoughtfully to the level of the baby squirrel in the cage. "Will Mr. Bell have to let him go eventually, back into the wild?'

Her dad shook his head. "He's not allowed to. It's against the law, I'm afraid. That's because he'd never survive out in the wild now. Poor little chap, it seems he'll have to make do with Ernie's backyard for the rest of his life!"

Mandy nodded.

"Don't worry, there are worse fates," Mr. Hope said.

"Oh, I know." But Mandy was still in a serious mood as she cycled over to school with the special kitten food. True, like Ernie Bell and the little squirrel, she was giving the kittens a chance of life. But without homes, would it be a life worth living?

She cycled and prayed that the notices in the post office, Animal Ark, and the village hall would work. She wondered too whether she could persuade Mr. Williams to give them a bit more time. A week was so

short! She leaned her bike against the hedge and went up the steps into the custodian's kitchen.

Once Walton was happily feeding, Mandy showed Mrs. Williams the new arrangements for Smoky, Patch, Amy, and Eric. To her surprise, the custodian's wife actually offered to help. "Don't tell my husband!" She pressed her thin lips tightly together. "He wouldn't approve!" She took Amy out of the basket and gingerly snuggled her up against her flowered apron, complete with feeding bottle. "Poor little scrap!" she murmured.

Mandy smiled. "She's fine. Look, she's hungry!"

Mrs. Williams sat happily while the kitten fed. "You mustn't mind my Eric," she confided. "I know he must seem like a grumpy old nuisance to you, but he's not so bad, really."

"No." Mandy tried to believe it. All she could think of were Mr. Williams's big boots and his loud voice. Hands as big as shovels. Temper like a volcano.

"You must think he's a stubborn old mule."

"No!" Mandy knew she didn't sound sincere.

"Yes!" Mrs. Williams looked down into the kitten's face. "Yes, you do. But he loves his garden!" She bent sideways towards Mandy. "Do you know, he keeps a squeeze bottle full of water out there on the porch. If a cat comes anywhere near his roses looking as if it's going to dig, Eric's out with the bottle, shooting at it. You should hear him when he scores a direct hit!'

"One wet cat!" Mandy joined in the laughter. "I was thinking he might give us a bit longer than a week," she said. "Even when we find homes for them, Walton will have to go on looking after them for quite a while. The less we need to move them around the better." She looked pleadingly at Mrs. Williams. "Maybe you could persuade him?"

"Hope by name, hopeful by nature!" Mrs. Williams said. But she was shaking her head. "No, I know Eric.

He's made up his mind!"

"Can't you just try?" Mandy was busy tidying up bottles and saucers.

But this time Mrs. Williams wouldn't bend. "No, it's not fair to him. He won't come into his own kitchen as it is. I know, I know," she interrupted Mandy's protest, "it's not sensible. But Eric's not always a sensible man. Who is? I'll tell you something else. He has a lot of pain, bending and kneeling and such. Arthritis. In the knees. Very painful." She lowered her voice. "To tell you the truth we don't mention it in case the school gets to hear. He's worried about his job!"

Mandy nodded. Suddenly Mr. Williams seemed human after all. "I'm sorry to hear that."

"Well, don't say I told you," Mrs. Williams warned. They were standing out on the porch. Walton was perched on the rim of the laundry basket licking herself clean. "He's out at his darts match this evening. It cheers him up."

Mrs. Williams stared up at the pebbled clouds. "But Eric's a worried man. It's the job, the house, everything. And the pain, of course. I can't even get him to go to a doctor." She glanced at Mandy. "So, you see, I can't ask him to do any more, can I? He's done enough already."

Mandy agreed and smiled sadly. She rode home slowly. She understood more about Mr. Williams's bad temper now, that was certain. But it didn't stop time passing. The sand was running steadily through the hourglass. They had five days left!

Five

"Hello, Welford 703267?" a woman's voice asked.

"This is it!" Mandy yelped, then lowered her voice to speak into the phone. "Yes, this is Welford 703267." She held her breath. "Who's speaking, please?" She gave her mother a hopeful thumbs up sign.

"Hello?" The voice sounded shy and cautious. There was a long pause.

"Hello, this is Amanda Hope. Who's speaking, please?" Mandy made a face of pretend panic at her mom.

"Hello, I want Welford 703267." The voice seemed

strange, and unused to the telephone.

"Can I help you, please?" Mandy said firmly. What was going on here? Her mom had paused over the washing up and was trying to listen in.

"Did you put a notice in the post office?" the woman on the end of the phone asked. "Are you the person with the kittens?"

"I am!" Mandy said with a grin. "I take it you're looking for a kitten?" Mrs. Hope winked and carried on with the breakfast dishes.

There was a long, crackly pause. "My name is Miss Marjorie Spry. I live at The Riddings. Please come to see me at two o'clock precisely."

Then the phone went dead.

"Well?" Mrs. Hope said.

Relief swept over her as Mandy realized that their plan was beginning to work. It was only nine o'clock on Saturday morning, and they'd already gotten a response! "Yes!" she yelled, nearly jumping for joy. "I'm off to tell Grandad!"

"Mandy, what if there are any more phone calls?' Mrs. Hope was drying her hands, following her out.

"Write down the numbers on that pad, will you, Mom? I'm so thrilled I can hardly wait!" She rushed up the lane without a jacket. It was drizzling, but she didn't care.

Her grandparents were stacking cans of soup inside the tiny cupboard aboard their camper. "Tomato, minestrone, cream of chicken!" Her gran handed them up to her grandad and ticked them off her list.

"Can opener?" Her grandfather popped his head out of the sliding door. He saw Mandy. "Hello, love!"

"It's worked! It's worked!" she greeted them. "Your brilliant card, Grandad, it's worked!"

He rubbed his hands. Mandy's grandparents both stood there in their twin knit sweaters, the drizzle wetting their gray hair. "Has it now? You have a response then?"

"Of course she has a response, haven't you, Mandy?" Gran put in. "Come inside. We're all getting wet."

"Who is it, then?" her grandad asked as he put on the kettle. "Anyone we know?"

"It's someone called Spy. No, Spry. That's it, Miss Marjorie Spry!"

Gran shut the kitchen door firmly and wiped her feet. Her head went on to one side. "The Riddings, isn't it?"

"Yes, The Riddings. Why, what's the matter? Do you know her?"

Her grandmother straightened herself up and bustled with the cups and saucers. "Yes. She lives at the big house out on Walton Road. Set back from the road. You know, the big old house!"

"I know!" Mandy said. They passed it every day on the way to school. It was well away from the traffic, with a huge lawn and garden. The perfect place for a cat to live! "She wants me to go and see her there at two o'clock this afternoon."

"Does she now?" her grandmother said. "That'll be one for the record book!"

"Why? What do you mean?" Mandy was nearly bursting with impatience. "I thought you'd be pleased!"

"We are, love," her grandad soothed.

"They're not usually keen on visitors, that's all," Gran explained. "In fact, I believe the last person they had over their threshold was Mr. Lovejoy, the old pastor before Mr. Walters, and that must be over five years ago!"

"No!" Mandy couldn't believe it.

"Yes, when their father died, the two sisters went into a sort of hibernation. It's true!" Gran insisted. "Still, that won't make any difference to you, I don't expect. If Miss Marjorie Spry wants to see you about a kitten and she's asked you along, you go and see her." She patted Mandy's hand. "They're harmless. A bit peculiar, but harmless enough."

"Anyway, it's best to check these places before you send these precious kittens off to their new homes," her grandad agreed. "You have to see if they're the right sort of thing!"

Mandy nodded, but she refused to be put off her stride.

"Take someone along with you," her grandad suggested. "Just to be on the safe side."

"James will come with me," Mandy said. She lifted a cardboard box full of bread, cornflakes, milk, and margarine. "Where do you want me to put these?"

Together they finished packing for "the great trial run," as her grandad called it. He meant their first expedition in their new camper. Finally they were ready.

"Map?" Grandad said, climbing into the driving seat.

"Map!" Gran produced it from the passenger shelf.

He turned on the windshield wipers. "Rubber boots? Storm capes? Rain hats?"

Gran flipped the map at him. "Ready?" she laughed. They waved to Mandy. "To sunny Scarborough!" she cried.

Mandy watched them disappear into the drizzle. There were still four hours to go before the visit to The Riddings. She would call James to arrange to meet him, then fill up the morning with little jobs at Animal Ark, and of course by cycling over to feed Walton and the kittens.

Two o'clock came at last. They arrived to find the front lawn of The Riddings spread out like a baseball field. James and Mandy decided to leave their bikes at the gate.

"I wonder who cuts this grass?" James said. It went in neat strips, light and dark. The edges were neatly clipped.

"I do!" An ancient man in corduroy trousers growled at them from behind a laurel hedge. He was bent almost double, probably from years and years of clipping the edges of huge lawns, Mandy guessed. "Have you come about a kitten?" he growled again.

They nodded.

"Miss Marjorie warned me about it. 'Geoffrey,' she said, 'show the girl up to the door!' So I'm following orders. This way!" He trudged ahead of them up the gravel driveway.

The house was as big as a hotel, built of stone, with pointed towers at each corner and battlements along the roof. It was covered in ivy. Though they passed it every day, James and Mandy could truly say that they'd never really paid much attention to it before. It had arched windows, stone pillars, and massive steps up to a wide front door. "Like a setting for a horror film!" Mandy whispered nervously.

Just when they felt they needed him most, their guide left them. "This is as far as I ever go. Ring three times," he said. "Nice and loud, mind. You might have to wait." And he went off, bowed and grumbling, to mow the lawn.

They looked at each other, shrugged, then James rang the bell. Silence. He rang again. And again. Finally someone began rattling locks on the other side of the massive door. "Wait!" a tiny voice ordered.

"What do you think we're doing?" James whispered to Mandy, trying not to laugh.

"Shh!" Mandy said. They had to be on their best behavior.

But even Mandy couldn't stop her jaw from hanging wide when the door finally creaked open.

The hall was the size of a ballroom, all in pink marble, with dark wood panels and glass chandeliers. But it was dull with age, and gray with years of neglect. What had once been as splendid as a fairytale had now decayed.

"Yes?" A lady stood before them. Her sticklike arms and legs poked out from a moth-eaten cream silk robe. She peered at them like a bat in the light.

"Miss Spry?" Mandy said uncertainly. A loud voice would have knocked the old lady down flat, she was sure.

"Yes!" She blinked her watery gray eyes. A skinny hand clutched the neck of her robe. "We don't see visitors!" she chattered.

Mandy's grandmother had been right. No one had stepped this way for years. Curtains were closed to keep out the daylight. A collection of old blue and white china ornaments cluttered the windowsills. Great piles of yellow newspapers were heaped on shelves. "Miss Marjorie Spry?" Mandy repeated, her heart sinking as her eyes took in the mess.

"Joan! Joan!" the woman shrieked. She began to close the door in their faces, but it was big and heavy. They saw the figure of another thin little woman come hurrying downstairs.

"Come in, come in," this second person ordered in a thin voice. She was beckoning to them, half running across the hall. "They've come about the kitten, Joan. Now open the door at once!"

And there they stood, two ladies thin as sticks, wild-haired, in matching silk robes. They had the same sharp faces. They had movements that

mirrored each other, and voices that echoed and mocked. Identical twins! Miss Joan and Miss Marjorie Spry!

"We don't want visitors!" the first one, Miss Joan, repeated with a birdlike twitch of her head.

"Yes, we do. I invited them!" Miss Marjorie argued. "I want a kitten for this dreadful old place. I want to bring some life in here!"

Miss Joan stared stubbornly, silently back at her sister. Her hand stayed poised to slam the door shut.

"I do, Joan! I'm tired of living in this old museum of a place. I want some life. We're not old yet; let's make a fresh start!" Miss Marjorie pleaded. "Look, this girl is advertising kittens. So let her in!"

At last Miss Joan gave way. Fascinated, Mandy and James stepped inside. To them it seemed like actually stepping into the past, into a kind of prison. Miss Joan pushed the door closed after them. It shut with a dull, heavy click. "What kittens?" Miss Joan challenged. She looked her sister in the face. "Who told me anything about a kitten?"

"I told you!" Miss Marjorie snapped. "An ad in the post office. Welford 703627!"

"But I don't like kittens!" Miss Joan protested. "You know that!"

Mandy stood in the middle of their argument, her

heart sinking right into her shoes by now. Miss Joan would never give in over this. Anyway, who'd want to leave a kitten where it wasn't wanted one hundred percent by everyone in the house? She looked at James and could tell that he thought the same. They both sighed.

They watched as Miss Marjorie grew more and more angry. "How do you know you don't like kittens?" Her eyes seemed to spark. "Have you had one? Have you ever owned a cat in your entire life? Have you? Have you?"

She turned to face Mandy and James, smoldering with rage. "*I* like cats! Joan likes cats, though she says she doesn't! She only says it to be awkward. Yes, you do!" she snapped at her twin. "She's just a spoilsport. It's because it's *my* idea to bring a kitten to The Riddings, to help bring the place back to life a bit. She says no to all my ideas!" She nearly cried with exasperation. The tiny twins stood face to face like featherweight boxers.

"Anyway, I'm the older twin!" Miss Marjorie said grandly. "And I have decided. Don't listen to her!"

"Well, they're still very young at present," Mandy began to explain. "We're only trying to find suitable homes for them in the future, you see." Still she couldn't settle those doubts about this being a good place to bring one of her precious kittens.

"Where is it?" The older twin began poking at Mandy and James as if a kitten might be hidden in one of their pockets.

"She's still with her mother. We're just starting to look, as I said."

"Not here? Not brought it with you?" Miss Marjorie said sharply.

"Ha, ha, ha!" Miss Joan sang out. She did a little dance of delight. "Ha, ha, ha!"

Miss Marjorie's thin patience finally snapped. "Quiet!" she bellowed. She picked up an old black umbrella from the stand and launched it like a javelin at her noisy sister. It missed by miles, but Miss Joan froze on the spot. Then she grabbed a newspaper from a shelf and rolled it up like a baseball bat. James and Mandy stood with their mouths open. Who would believe them?

"Joan!" Miss Marjorie warned.

"You threw something at me first!" Miss Joan retaliated.

"Get out!" Miss Marjorie cried. "Get out, get out!"

James and Mandy didn't know if she meant them or her sister. Everything was chaos. Mandy was growing sure of just one thing, though: this was no place for a tiny kitten.

She knew this once and for all when Miss Joan, in her mischief, raised her rolled newspaper and began to chase Miss Marjorie from the hall into the study, a room at the front of the house. In a panic to stop them from injuring each other, Mandy and James hurried after.

Mandy stopped short. The room was lined from ceiling to floor with old books. But on the many tables scattered about the room were glass cases, dozens of them. Inside the dusty cases, perched, poised, and perfectly preserved, were . . . stuffed animals!

A heron stood on one leg, forever fishing. An otter bared his teeth at an invisible enemy. A wildcat stared warily out, as if he knew he was about to be made extinct in Britain. Mandy squealed. Both hands flew to her cheeks.

"Let's go!" James said. For once, he took the lead. He grabbed her hand and made a run for it, back through the littered hall. They didn't turn to see if they were being followed. They just ran.

"Hey, you two!" Miss Marjorie called.

But they covered the distance to the gate in record time, ignoring the grinning gardener as they fled. Outside the gate they paused for breath. "Well?" James gasped.

"No good," Mandy said, almost in tears. The door was closed; the ivy still smothered the walls. The house seemed empty and grim. It would be another five years before anyone dared to disturb it.

"I agree." They were both too shocked to think straight.

It was only the routine of cycling over to look after things in the Williamses' kitchen that saved them. They fed the kittens and cycled home to news from Mandy's mom.

Mrs. Hope smiled across the treatment table where she was putting Snap the terrier to sleep. "A Mrs. Parker Smythe has been on the phone," she said. "She says she's interested in one of the kittens!"

Six

Mandy was up early the next day. She'd done her chores, been over to feed Walton, and was back before her mom had finished breakfast.

"I'll take you up to the Parker Smythes in the car, if you like," Mrs. Hope offered. "The arrangement was for nine-thirty." It was the only other phone call about the kittens since the Misses Spry disaster, so Mandy felt glad her mother was coming along to give moral support.

"It's way out of the village, up by the Beacon." Mrs. Hope opened the passenger door of their big four-wheel-drive. "Hop in," she said. "Do we have to call for James as well?"

"No. He came over earlier to feed the kittens, but he has a football match today, and his mom told him to take Blackie on an extra long walk, so he can't come."

"Do the Hunters still have that cat of theirs?" Mrs. Hope fastened her seat belt.

"Benji? Yes, of course. Why?"

"He's getting a bit old, that's all."

They took the high road out of Welford. Soon a steep hill loomed ahead of them. On top there was a stone pillar, visible for miles around: the Beacon.

"I guess James is still recovering from yesterday?" Mrs. Hope said, her eyes set firmly on the road ahead. She went rapidly down the gears.

Mandy nodded. "We both are." Mandy was brave, but even she was rattled by the Spry sisters. She reckoned she was the least squeamish person around; she'd watched operations on stomachs, intestines, legs, and hearts. But she shuddered at the memory of the poor stuffed creatures in the library at The Riddings, glass-eyed, covered in dust.

"You have to remember it was the fashion a hundred years ago. Most people have thrown those glass cases full of birds and animals away by now. But don't blame the twins too much. Poor things." Mrs.

Hope spoke quietly. She pushed a stray strand of hair behind her ear.

"Yes," Mandy agreed. "Animals look so much better alive and out in the wild, not stuffed inside some rotten case!"

"I meant the sisters!" Her mom glanced across at her. The hill was beginning to flatten out now. They could see the Beacon just ahead. "They don't mean anyone any harm."

"What, those two horrible old things! Nobody ever goes near them, and all they ever do is argue!"

"Exactly," Mrs. Hope said softly.

And Mandy had to sit and think about that one as they pulled up outside a high hawthorn hedge with double iron gates, electronically controlled. "Beacon House" was written in big gold letters. And "No Parking. Trespassers will be prosecuted."

Mrs. Hope put on the handbrake. "Anyway, this looks more straightforward." She spoke into a little security box on the gatepost, then the gate opened as if by magic.

Mandy turned and took in the long-distance view of the valley: its odd-shaped patchwork fields, scattered hillside farms, the road and river running parallel along the bottom, and Welford's two main streets crisscrossing in the far distance.

Then she turned again and followed her mother up the drive. They went on foot through a small bluebell wood, up to the big white house.

"What's that?" Mandy whispered. She pointed to a flat paved area the size of a tennis court, but marked with large white circles. It wasn't a tennis court anyway, because that was on the other side, to the right of the house.

"Helicopter pad?" Mrs. Hope suggested. She rang the doorbell.

Mandy gulped. A very blonde, very smart woman opened the door. She was dressed in white shirt and trousers, with gold necklaces, rings, bracelets. A lot of gold. Even her shoes had gold decorations sewn on.

Mandy felt her mother give her a little shove forward to speak. "Mrs. Parker Smythe?" she asked nervously.

The woman nodded. Her blonde hair stayed put. Not a highlighted strand moved. Her smile revealed two rows of perfectly even, perfectly white teeth between shiny pink lips. "Come in!" she said, like you heard it said in posh films, usually with "darling" on the end.

They went in and she closed the door. "Come this way!" she said, all teeth and lipstick, and gold bits dangling. Through the white hall with Italian tiles and rugs, into the kitchen. "You must be Mandy? You put the nice pink ad in the village hall? I was picking up Imogen from the Brownies and we saw your notice!' she gushed.

Mandy nodded. She was finding it hard to fit in a word. Anyway, the kitchen made her feel that being there in her jeans and T-shirt and talking out loud in her ordinary voice was a bit of a mistake. It wasn't a bit like the old pine table and quarry-tiled floor of her own kitchen. This had shiny blue glass bowls and white gadgets everywhere, and no food anywhere to be seen.

Mrs. Parker Smythe didn't seem to notice Mandy's shyness. "Imogen is my little girl. She's seven!" she said proudly, as if Imogen being seven was like winning the Olympic Games singlehanded.

"And this is Ronald, my husband. He's in satellite television!"

A balding man walked in, nodded and walked out again. He wore the palest yellow V-neck sweater and tan checked trousers.

"He's going to play golf," Mrs. Parker Smythe told them. She shared another confidence: "With Jason Shaw! You know, Jason Shaw, the actor! They're very good friends, Ronald and Jason!"

Mandy risked a glance at her mother but didn't dare ask, "Jason who?" Her mother was looking steadily out of the window, trying not to smile.

"We first met Jason when he came to film here, you know," Mrs. Parker Smythe rattled on. "For an episode of *The Swallows in Spring,* this time last year. They used our swimming pool!"

Mandy gulped again. She couldn't help it. Maybe tough little Smoky would be the right kitten for the Parker Smythes. The rough-and-tumble one. He'd bring them down to earth.

"Yes, our swimming pool was used as a set for the program. It belongs to the right period for the series. So Jason and the crew came up. That's how we met!" Mrs. Parker Smythe bubbled on. She seemed to have forgotten all about the reason for their visit.

"Did you want a kitten for your little girl?" Mandy managed to fit in at last. Mr. Parker Smythe wandered in and out again, apparently looking for something.

"Yes, well, we have so much space here." Mrs. Parker Smythe spread her arms and her jewelry jangled. "And such a big garden! And of course we have security cameras out there, so there's no danger of the poor little mite getting lost or anything!"

Mandy noticed her mother's eyebrows shoot up a fraction of an inch.

"And when we're away at our house in Tuscany, we still have Mrs. Bates, our housekeeper, to come in and look after the kitten, feed it and so on." Mrs. Parker Smythe looked at her gold watch. "Would you please excuse me a moment?" She dashed off after her husband.

"I wonder what he's lost," Mandy whispered.

"His helicopter?" her mom said. But no; they heard huge blades begin to whir out on the pad. Clearly it had been wheeled out from its hangar and prepared for takeoff.

They grinned. Mandy felt more relaxed. "What if Smoky doesn't fit in here because he's only a plain, ordinary tomcat?"

"Let's meet the little girl first, before we make any decisions," Mrs. Hope said.

Mandy nodded. She had to admit, once again, the signs were not all that promising.

"Oh, good, you're still here!" Mrs. Parker Smythe floated back in after a few minutes. "Now you must come through. Come and meet Imogen!"

She led them out of the kitchen across a giant sunroom full of artificial palms and pink-flowered cane furniture. But this was only a link to the house's main attraction, its indoor heated pool. This opened up from the sunroom through wide double doors.

The poolside was dazzling white and the water was deep blue. There was a fountain at one end, and windows from ceiling to floor all down one side. And there in the water, swimming like a walrus with just its nose and whiskers out of the water, was Imogen Parker Smythe.

"Imogen!" her mother called, clapping her jewelled hands smartly.

Imogen ignored her.

"Imogen, we have visitors!" her mother called again.

No response. Imogen swam round and round the fountain at the deep end. Mandy was amazed by her rudeness. *I'd never get away with that!* she thought.

Mrs. Parker Smythe sighed. "Come along, we'd better go down." She went along the poolside carrying an apricot-colored bathrobe and a towel for her daughter. Mandy and Mrs. Hope followed.

"Imogen!" Mrs. Parker Smythe said in a coaxing voice. She crouched beside the water. "Now come along, darling. Come and talk to Mommy about a sweetie, itsy bitsy little kittie for Immikins!"

Mandy swallowed hard. She stuck both hands into her jeans pockets. *Yuk!* she thought. She just hoped no one could read her mind.

"Won't!" Imogen retorted, swimming in smaller circles.

"Oh, come on, darling! Remember, we talked about a sweet little furry kitty for you just this morning at breakfast. Remember?"

"No!" Imogen spat out water like a whale.

"Immie!" Mrs. Parker Smythe was getting wet. "Now come along out of there immediately, or I'll call your daddy!"

With a great sigh and much splashing, Imogen Parker Smythe heaved herself out of the water. She was a mousy-haired, slightly overweight little girl with a constant scowl. She squirmed as her mother wrapped her in the bathrobe. She pushed away the towel offered for her dripping hair. Instead she shook her head from side to side like a dog.

"Hello," Mandy said. She forced herself to take the lead in this conversation.

Imogen tossed her head and sniffed up great drips of water.

"I hear you want a kitten?" Mandy went on.

Sniff. Sniff.

"I've got four kittens. Four tiny ones just a few days old. But soon their mother will finish feeding them, and after that they'll need really good names

and somebody to look after them!" Mandy explained in what she thought was a clear, sensible way.

"I know that!" Imogen snorted. "Everyone knows that!"

"Immie!" Mrs. Parker Smythe chirped.

"They'll need good homes, and someone very kind and careful to look after them!" Mandy said in a much cooler voice.

"What color are they?" Imogen demanded, eye to eye with Mandy. "I want a white one!"

Mandy paused. "Well, the color isn't that important, really, is it? I mean, a kitten isn't a kind of toy, is it? It's a real live animal, you know. Soon it'll grow into a big cat that will still need feeding and taking to the vet, and somewhere clean and airy to sleep. In fact, it will need lots of looking after!"

Imogen turned to her mother. "I only want a white one!" she whined.

"But Immikins!" Mrs. Parker Smythe looked helplessly at Mandy.

"You said I could have a white one!" The child stamped her foot. "A white kitten! A fluffy white one with long fur! I want one! I want one!"

Mandy was furious. She felt like stepping right up to the revolting girl and pushing her back into the swimming pool. "Kittens are not toys!" she repeated. "And they don't have to match your color scheme!"

"Mandy!" Mrs. Hope warned under her breath.

But Imogen was equal to the fight. She took a long look at Mandy, then she screwed her face tight and whined loudly. "O-o-oh, Mommy, make the horrible nasty girl go away! I don't like her! Make her go away, Mommy!"

Mrs. Parker Smythe fell for it. "There, there, Immikins, don't cry!" she said. She cuddled her daughter at a distance, so as to keep dry. "You don't have to have a kitty if you don't want one, darling. There, there!"

Mandy saw Imogen's face peep out at her from behind pudgy little fists. Imogen sneered up at her. "That got you!" she seemed to be saying.

Mrs. Hope was pulling at Mandy's arm. "Time to go," she urged.

But Mrs. Parker Smythe had left off cuddling Imogen and came towards them. "Take no notice," she whispered. "Imogen's in one of her moods. You can bring the kitten anyway. I'll talk her into it."

But Mandy stood her ground. She was determined to have her say. "Mrs. Parker Smythe," she announced, "I'm afraid this would never work!"

Mrs. Parker Smythe's gold jewelry trembled as she went back and bent over her daughter.

Mandy continued. "To keep a pet you have to be a sensible, caring person. Animals have rights, you know, and one of those rights is to belong to a good, responsible owner!" She paused for breath, but there was no stopping her now. "And I'm afraid Imogen just doesn't qualify! I couldn't imagine anyone *less* suited to look after Smoky, Patch, Amy, or Eric!"

She glared down at them as they hugged each other by the side of their swanky pool. She turned on her heel. Her sneakers squeaked on the wet tiles all the way down to the French doors, but she didn't care. She swung through the sunroom, the designer kitchen, the hall. Mrs. Hope caught up with her halfway down the driveway.

"Sorry, Mom, for being rude." Mandy said. But her mother didn't seem to mind as they marched out to the car, shoulder to shoulder.

"No good," Mrs. Hope sighed and opened the door.

Mandy sank back in the passenger seat. She felt bitter about spoiled little rich kids and their soft mothers. And she was panicking about the kittens. Two replies to their ads so far, and two disastrous results! "No, no good again!" she said.

Tears of disappointment threatened, but she bit

them back. She had to keep on looking. She had to succeed!

Seven

The weekend was almost over, and still the kittens were homeless. Mr. Williams would kick them out of his kitchen on Thursday, or do something dreadful. For him, they weren't creatures with feelings. They were just nuisances to be gotten rid of.

"That's how some people think," Mandy's dad explained. "Especially some older people around here. You don't get sentimental about animals when you live on farms or in the villages. When Mr. Williams was young, they drowned unwanted kittens in the rain barrel behind the barn. I don't suppose they even thought it was cruel."

Mandy shuddered. As far as she was concerned, it was murder.

"Come on, help me take this young chap over to Ernie's!" Mr. Hope suggested. He picked up the plastic cage containing the baby squirrel. "I've checked him over and he's as right as rain. He can go into the run at the back of Ernie's house and we'll see how he gets along."

They set off on foot down their lane to the main street. It was a sunny afternoon, with blossoms everywhere. Gardeners were out with their trowels and pruners, making the flowers stand at attention. "Good afternoon," people said pleasantly. Some stopped to look at the squirrel and pass the time of day.

Mandy liked the fact that everyone knew her father. He'd been born up at Lilac Cottage and had lived in Welford all his life, except for his college days in York. The older villagers still called him "young Adam" or "Tom Hope's lad." They knew he was a brainy boy, he'd been to college, and he was known as a decent vet. At any rate, he was one of them.

The women came out of their houses and made a fuss over Mandy, while the men described problems with moles on their lawns, or a sheep stuck in the cattle fence at the back of the Janekis' farm. The squirrel scampered in its cage, accepting offers of peanuts through the grille.

At last Mandy and her father reached the Fox and Goose. "It's only taken us an hour and fifteen minutes!" she remarked.

Mr. Hope laughed and went into the tavern for half a pint of beer and a can of cold soda for Mandy. They spent another fifteen minutes in the last rays of sunshine, sitting on a bench, gossiping.

"Right!" Mr. Hope wiped his beard clean of any stray froth and stood up. He sounded purposeful at last. "You bring the squirrel, Mandy."

She followed him across the cobbled courtyard of the pub. The squirrel scuttled in its cage.

"That used to be the forge," Mr. Hope said. He pointed to the plush restaurant at the side of the pub.

"I know, Dad, you've told me!"

He carried on regardless. "My own grandfather had the place in the 1920s."

"I know, Dad!" Boy, was he embarrassing sometimes. Mandy shuffled from one foot to the other. Soon she'd have to cycle over to Walton for the regular evening feed. The kittens were doing well on the special liquid food, and Walton herself was looking sleeker. Mandy was pleased with their progress. "Come on, Dad, let's go!"

He turned and grinned. "Sorry, love!" And he led the way again, down the side of the pub to a row of tiny two-story stone cottages that had seen better days. There were five cottages, all with beaten-up doors, unruly ivy, and great stone slabs making a pathway along the length of the row. Most of the front doors stood open in the sunshine.

"Now then, young Adam!" a gruff voice said.

Mandy and Mr. Hope stopped at the first house. She might have known they wouldn't make it to Ernie's without at least two more interruptions.

"Hello, Walter. Lovely day!" Mr. Hope stopped and leaned in at Walter Pickard's door. "How are things?"

"Mustn't grumble," the old man said. "Now then, young miss!"

Mandy smiled hello. Walter never remembered the name of anyone under thirty. It was just "young miss" or "young sir." He was a retired butcher, a Wednesday evening church bell-ringer alongside her grandad, and, what's more, a cat lover! Two lovely old ginger cats sunned themselves on his front doorstep.

"What have we here?" Walter said, bending and tapping the cage. Inside, the squirrel sat up and begged. "Hey up!" Walter said, half laughing. He went off down the dark, narrow hallway and came back with a piece of cracker, which he fed to the squirrel.

Mandy liked Walter. He was a big man, but his deep voice was gentle, and his lined face under its flat cloth cap was always smiling. His wife had died last year, but Walter's three cats still kept him company. Mandy liked him because of his smile and his cats. What she couldn't understand was how he'd spent his entire working life in a butcher's shop. All those cold sides of beef hanging on their hooks. All those dead chickens. Mandy shuddered. She was glad she was a vegetarian. These days she hardly ever ate meat.

Mr. Hope glanced at his watch. "Do you know if Ernie's in?" he asked.

Walter nodded. "Most likely."

"In that case I'll just pop this little fellow along to him." Mr. Hope picked up the cage, saw Mandy was busy stroking the ginger cats and said, "I'll leave you here, Mandy, to tell Walter the story of Ernie Bell and the orphan squirrel!" Then he wandered off down the row.

Mandy recounted the sad story of the squirrel.

"Ernie Bell!" Walter said, shaking his head. "He's adopting a squirrel, that miserable old devil!" It was like saying he, Walter Pickard, had won the football pools.

Mandy had her hand deep in the soft, warm fur of one of the old ginger cats when an idea struck her. She looked up from her cross-legged position on the path. "Walter, how many cats do you have?" she asked casually. But the excitement of the idea was beginning to make her heart beat faster.

"Three," he said. He sat down heavily on an old wooden stool just inside the doorway. "That one's called Scraps because she feeds on any scraps I give her. She's not the least bit fussy." He pointed to the one Mandy was stroking. "And that's Missie over there, because she's a proper little madam, and only eats the best fish and chicken breast." This other ginger cat was contentedly purring in the sun. "Then there's Tom. He's indoors at present."

Mandy listened quietly, but she thought furiously.

"We used to have another one, you know," Walter went on. "My Mary loved cats, and it was her favorite, Susie, that passed away just after Christmas." He sat with his own memories for a while, then pulled himself together. "Susie was a dainty little cat, just like my Mary. That's why she was her favorite." He smiled. "Yes, indeed."

Mandy nodded. She knew it was now or never.

"Why not get another?" she said. "It just so happens I'm looking for homes for kittens right now, and there's one little dainty one, a little tortoiseshell called Amy, who'd be just right for you, I'm sure!"

Walter listened. He seemed to like the idea. "A tortoiseshell?"

"Yes. They're only a few days old, and we're partly having to hand-rear them, James Hunter and me, because the mother's too weak. She was a stray. But we'll need homes for all of them. Good homes!" She stressed the "good" and looked up at Walter.

He blew out his cheeks like a trumpeter. "A tortoiseshell?" he repeated. Mandy pictured a young kitten scampering about on the warm flagstones all summer long, jumping up at his wallflowers, tumbling in over the step.

"A really lovely little tortoiseshell!" she insisted. She held her breath.

"Aye, I'd love one," Walter sighed.

"Oh, it'd be a perfect home for Amy!" Mandy told him. "It's nice and quiet back here, off the road, and the older cats would look after her, and you know all about kittens. It would be ideal!"

Say yes, she prayed. *Say yes!*

But a shadow crept down the hallway. A big bruiser of a shadow padding up to the doorstep

in the sinister shape of Tom.

"Hello!" Mandy said to the barrel-shaped cat. He stood foursquare in his doorway. He bared his teeth and hissed. "Hello there!" She ran her fingers up and down the flagstones. "Come here!" she coaxed. He ignored her game. Sulkily he padded across the step, back and forth, strong shouldered, wide mouthed. He was a black and white bully with a pirate's black patch over his left eye, a chewed left ear and ragged whiskers.

"Ah, Tom!" Walter said with a sigh of regret.

Tom arched his back at Mandy and spat. He padded around the two ginger females, just checking up on them. Then he stood and stared again at Mandy.

"There's Tom to consider, you see," Walter explained. "Scraps and Missie would be fine. But not

Tom." The old man shook his head. "Just take one look at him. He'd eat a new kitten for breakfast!"

Mandy could believe it. Never had she seen a cat like Tom; a heavyweight, a bouncer, a sumo wrestler of a cat!

"No," Walter said sadly. "Much as I'd like to, I'm afraid old Tom wouldn't be happy with a stranger about the place. You can see my problem?"

Mandy nodded. Though she was desperate, she had to agree.

"Never mind, Thomas, no one's going to come upsetting you." Walter bent forward to scratch the chewed-up old ear. "Just relax, old chap!"

The cat blinked and tilted its colossal head in victory. He'd staked out his territory and won.

Sadly Mandy got to her feet. Such a missed opportunity! But her dad was returning with the empty cage. "Ready?" he asked.

They said their goodbyes to Walter and set off across the pub yard. The old man continued to sit on his stool, cats at his feet.

"I say," Mr. Hope said, glancing backwards, "Old Walter's fond of cats. Why don't you—"

"It's all right, Dad," Mandy interrupted, "I already have. I asked him and he says he'd like another kitten, but Thomas the Terrible wouldn't appreciate it." She joked, but she was feeling very low. "In the end he said no."

"Ah, well," Mr. Hope said, swinging the empty cage, lost in his own thoughts.

All the gardeners had gone inside for tea, so their walk home was much quieter and quicker. Mrs. Hope had prepared their own evening meal, knowing that Mandy would want to cycle over to school before it got dark. No one mentioned the kittens. If they had, Mandy felt she might have broken down. And her mom and dad knew when not to fuss. She ate, then packed her bag. She met James at the post office, and together they cycled to Walton.

Mr. Williams was in a very bad mood.

"It's Sunday night," Mrs. Williams reminded them. "He always gets like this on a Sunday night."

He'd been stamping about the kitchen when they arrived, but as soon as he saw them, he grunted, took his Sunday newspaper and headed out of the room.

"It's because it's Monday tomorrow," Mrs. Williams explained. "W-O-R-K! The dreaded four-letter word."

Then Tuesday, then Wednesday, Mandy thought with a lurch. She wanted to stop the clock, or at least to stretch the days. The trouble was, as each visit to the kittens came and went, she grew fonder of them. They were about five inches long and weighed just three or four ounces or so. They hadn't yet struggled to their feet, and their eyes were still closed. Smoky was strongest, but Patch gave him a good scrap in their fight for food, while Amy and Eric were patient, more content.

Now was the time to ask Mrs. Williams if they could gently tip the laundry basket onto its side so the kittens could begin to sniff the daylight of their own accord. "And then Walton might be ready to move them to a new nest," Mandy suggested.

"What, tip it over and leave it there?" Mrs. Williams asked. She looked doubtful. "It'd make the place look a terrible mess!" But in the end she agreed. The basket could be tipped onto its side.

As James and Mandy fed each of the kittens in turn, Mr. Williams stamped back in. He was wearing a very clean, very stiff white shirt and a maroon tie. He looked smart in his dark suit, but he walked awkwardly, Mandy noticed for the first time. He frowned at the upturned laundry basket.

Mrs. Williams leapt to her feet. She was ready for church, in her beige dress and silk scarf. "Now, Eric!" she warned. She saw him glaring at the two kittens who happened to be pulling by mistake at the sleeve of his best blue shirt. They were seeking out Walton, but getting tangled in the shirt instead. "It's only till Wednesday night!" she promised.

He didn't even grunt. He just stamped out onto the porch.

"Good thing it's Sunday!" Mrs. Williams whispered.

"Why?" James asked.

"Eric never swears on a Sunday," she said. She raised her eyebrows. "Otherwise the air in the kitchen would be blue as that shirt!" She sighed as she picked up her shiny brown handbag. She checked her keys. "Lock the door when you go," she reminded them. Then she followed her husband down the road to church.

Mandy shook her head. The kittens were all safe for the night. James was washing Walton's feeding bowl and saucer, and the mother cat was coming to Mandy for a final grateful stroke before she settled down with her kittens. "I wish . . ." Mandy said. But she never finished the sentence.

James felt helpless too as they checked the kitchen, turned off the light, and locked the door. "That's what I like about computers," he said out of the blue as they pulled up out of town on their bikes.

"Huh?" Mandy said. "What are you talking about?" James sometimes came out with these odd things.

"Computers. That's what I like about them. They're straightforward and simple, and they never make you feel bad."

"Not like people and animals, you mean?"

He nodded. "And you can just switch them on and off, no problem."

They cycled for a while in silence.

"But they go wrong!" Mandy objected. You shouldn't prefer machines to live things, surely.

"So do animals," he said. Another silence. "Like Benji."

"Oh, what's wrong with Benji?" Mandy asked. James had had Benji for as long as she could remember; he was a lovely, docile black tomcat.

"Dunno," James said. "My mom has to bring him into the Ark tomorrow morning to see if they can find out."

Mandy nodded and sighed. "Well, see you tomorrow, early?" she said by way of goodbye.

"Tomorrow early," James promised, as they each rode their separate ways.

Eight

One little victory would be enough, Mandy thought. One home for one kitten. It wasn't asking much, and it would be a start. She went through the names they'd had so far, just to make sure that none of them would do.

Thinking hard, she passed Simon a thermometer to take the temperature of a Border collie who was just recovering from parvovirus. It was only because she was so young and strong that she'd survived.

Simon stroked the dog's long, black coat. "At least they'll remember to have her vaccinated from now on," he said.

Mandy nodded, but she was thinking of Miss Marjorie Spry. Surely even she could remember to open a can of cat food each day. The kitten could be given a quiet, cozy corner in the garden shed if that old gardener would clear a space. Mandy stopped scooping meat into the dog bowls and stood, fork poised.

"A penny for them," Simon said with a smile. He was looking at his watch.

"What?" Mandy was imagining Amy snugly tucked up behind the old flowerpots and garden shears.

"A penny for your thoughts!" Simon took the fork and went on preparing bowls of food for their resident cocker spaniel and two black Labradors. "You don't usually daydream on the job!" he said.

"Oh, sorry!" Mandy gave a sigh. Of course, The Riddings wasn't any good. Simon had broken her dream. She recalled the frozen snarl of the stuffed wildcat, the hopeful glass stare of the heron. All those dusty cases with dead animals in them. She feared it would never work to send Amy there, and the poor kitten was still homeless.

"Best get a move on," Simon said. "Here, you do the hamster dishes next, while I clean out the cages. And remember Flopsy and company out back!"

Mandy took the scoop full of rabbit food out into the backyard. There was always the Parker Smythe mansion for Smoky, she told herself. She knew she was clutching at straws, though. How long would it be before the kitten lost its novelty? Two days? Mandy sighed again. And that was only if Imogen would accept a gray cat. No, she wouldn't wish Imogen Parker Smythe on her worst enemy, let alone on precious Smoky.

If only Walter Pickard's old tomcat had been better tempered! Mandy stood there with a handful of oats and sunflower seed mixture, deep in thought.

When she went inside, Simon had finished the hamster cages. He took a last look at her, and in his quiet way took charge. "Look," he said, "I'll finish here. I thought you had to get off to school early again."

"What? Oh, yes, thanks!" Mandy dusted down her hands and scrambled out of her white coat. "Is that the time? I must run!"

She was out of Animal Ark and in her school uniform when she bumped into her mom on the stairs. "Any phone calls?" she asked, hoping for more responses to the ads.

"No," Mrs. Hope said.

"Right." She hadn't really expected any this time. Her hopes were not high.

Then she was out of the house, up the lane to meet James outside McFarlane's. Her mind was still working overtime. *I suppose I could always try Walter again,* she thought as she screeched to a halt. James was already there.

"Sorry I'm late!" she said.

James was quieter than usual as they cycled over, but Mandy had a lot on her mind, too.

School went by in a semi-daze. She got two questions wrong in history, and a lecture from Mr. Holmes. "What's wrong, Amanda? This isn't like you. Been watching too much television, I expect. Now just pay attention, please!" Mandy went red and hot, and tried to concentrate.

She was thinking of the kittens when a group of friends asked her if she was going to the disco on Friday. Mandy didn't answer. "Oh, be like that!" one said. They were all giggling about something or other. "Don't think we care whether you come or not! You're not the center of the universe, Mandy Hope!" And they flounced off.

Mandy shrugged. It was time to go and feed the kittens.

And she was still thinking of them when James

came up after school and told her quietly that he had to go straight home tonight. He'd promised his mom specially.

Mandy nodded. "See you tomorrow then," she said. She had a plan in her head; not much of a plan, but she'd decided she would visit Walter again. She'd feed the kittens first, then she'd call in at the cottages. Anyway, it couldn't do any harm. She'd invent an excuse; maybe she'd visit Ernie Bell's squirrel and just "happen" to call in on Walter. He mustn't think she was pestering on purpose.

"Hello, young miss!" Walter greeted her from his open door. "Where's that grandad of yours gone? I haven't seen him around here lately."

Mandy propped her bike against the end wall. "Hi, Walter." She tried to sound casual. "He's off touring in his new van." She gave him one of her cheeriest smiles. It was an effort, but she wanted to be bright and breezy.

"Camping!" Walter said with a low whistle. "At their age!"

"Not exactly." She explained the luxuries of the modern mobile home. "It has a fridge, electricity, everything!"

"Hmph! Don't they have a fridge and electricity at their house?"

"Yes."

"Well, then, what's the point?" Walter said. His ginger cats came padding elegantly down the hall.

Mandy gave in and changed the subject. She stroked Scraps and Missie. "I've just popped by to see Mr. Bell's squirrel," she said casually. "To see if he's settled in okay."

Walter nodded. "Yes, if he'll see you," he said. "Ernie doesn't always answer his door!"

"I'll be back in a minute," she said.

She walked up the flagstone path to the end of the row. She knocked hard. The green door was faded and flaking; it needed a good coat of paint. And it had an old lion knocker that hadn't been cleaned for years. It was stiff with disuse. She knocked again.

"Hold your horses, hold your horses!" Ernie grumbled from inside. She heard bolts sliding, locks turning. Finally Ernie opened his front door.

Mandy heard Walter mumble and turn back inside his own house. She was left to face Ernie alone.

"Yes?" Ernie snapped. He was a small man with a shock of straight white hair rising back from his lined forehead. There was something birdlike about his sharp nose, his bright, dark eyes. He wore an old vest and a shirt without a collar. "Yes?" he said again, peering at Mandy.

She introduced herself as the vet's daughter. "My dad brought back the squirrel yesterday. How is he?" she asked.

Ernie frowned. "Fine, fine. What do you want now? You can't have him back, you know. I've paid the bill!"

"No, I don't want to take him back," Mandy tried to explain.

"Good. It cost me a fortune just to have him checked over, I can tell you. But I paid!" he insisted. He stood there, frowning.

"No, I—" Mandy hesitated, then changed tactics. "What's his name?" she asked.

Ernie paused. "Sammy," he said, as if he didn't want anyone to hear. "All right?"

"Yes, it's a nice name. I was just wondering, could I take a look at him, please?"

She waited until Ernie made up his mind. He stared at her, thought a while, then nodded. "This way," he said at last.

He led her down a dark passage, through his kitchen and out into the backyard. Four gardens along the way, Walter was out in his garden. He leaned his forearms against his fence top. "Now then,

Ernie!" he greeted his unfriendly neighbor.

Ernie grunted. He stood by, watching suspiciously as Mandy inspected the squirrel run.

"Sammy!" Mandy called gently. There was a sturdy hutch at the far end of the run, with a small hole for an entrance, which only something as tiny and agile as a squirrel could use. The little creature poked out its round gray head.

"Here," Ernie said. "Tempt him with these!" He handed Mandy a few peanuts from his trouser pocket.

And Sammy bounded out of the hutch. He clung upside-down to the netting, swinging like a trapeze artist towards her. His feet never touched the ground.

Mandy held out the nuts in the palm of her hand. Delicately Sammy watched, reached out a paw and snatched the food. He swung away to a safe distance, then nibbled.

Mandy studied him. This was only the second time she'd been this close to a squirrel. The run was ten yards long, made of timber and fine mesh. Very safe. "This is great!" she told Ernie, tapping the framework.

"Hmm." Ernie nodded. "So it should be." He too was watching the squirrel, and his face had lost its

frown. "I've had a fair bit of practice, mind you. I was a carpenter for more than fifty years!" Then as if he'd given away top secret information, his mouth clamped shut and the frown returned.

"Well, it's great," Mandy said. "Really sturdy and safe. I'm glad Sammy's found such a good home!" It was almost enough to take her mind off homeless kittens. But she could see Walter along there in his own yard, and she was desperate to talk with him. She remembered her real purpose: to persuade Walter and old Tom to change their minds. "Can I come and visit Sammy again?" she asked Ernie.

He swallowed hard, but he nodded slowly. "You can call again," he agreed. "It might not always suit me to answer the door, you understand. But you can always try."

He followed her out to the front of the house. "Well, Mr. Bell!" Mandy was about to turn and thank him again for showing her the squirrel, but the flaky green door was already closed. And like a figure in a Swiss cuckoo clock, Walter was already out at his own front door. As usual, he was not minding his own business.

Mandy wandered towards him. She was going to ask, "How's old Tom today?" and then gently add that perhaps Tom would take to a new kitten, if they introduced him to the idea gradually.

But Walter must have been a mind reader. She never got any further than "How's old Tom?" before he cut her short.

"It's no good you wheedling away, young miss!" Walter laughed at her surprise. "I know what you're going to ask, and Tom's answer is still no!"

As if to confirm this, Tom came barreling around the corner at top speed and bashed right into Mandy's bike. Down it crashed. Tom wailed loudly, leaped over the spinning wheels, and vanished across the pub yard.

"See!" Walter said, laughing again. He picked up the bike. "Nothing's safe with our Tom on the scene!" He turned to Mandy, then he looked down the row to Ernie's end house. "But you know something, I think we've just had an idea!"

"We have?" To Mandy it didn't feel as if anything was going right.

"Yes. You hit it off with old Ernie, didn't you?" Walter scratched his head, a sure sign that he was thinking.

"I suppose so," Mandy said doubtfully. "Listen, you don't think I should ask him!" Her eyes lit up. "I mean, you mean I should ask him to take a kitten!" She felt the idea light up all the dark corners of her mind.

But Walter was shaking his head. "No, no, I don't think you should ask him exactly!"

Mandy's face fell again. "Why not? He likes animals. He rescued little Sammy, didn't he?"

"Yes, but Ernie would say no if you asked him directly. On principle, he always says no. He's a grumpy, cantankerous old so-and-so, is Ernie."

Mandy had to agree. "So what's our idea?" she asked.

"It's this!" Walter got into a huddle with Mandy around the corner, out of sight.

The idea involved taking a very big risk. But then Mandy had forty-eight hours to solve four very big problems. She listened to Walter, she nodded, she considered it. She thought of Sammy snug in his custom-built hutch. She decided to risk it.

So she called home and said she'd be late. Then she rode back over to Walton.

Mrs. Williams watched with concern as Mandy gave Amy a special feeding and tucked her into a specially lined cardboard box. Amy peered up, unseeing, sniffed, then settled down. Walton came over, glanced in, looked up at Mandy, then retreated to the laundry basket. She sat quietly inside with her other three kittens, looking out.

"She trusts you!" Mrs. Williams said. "Poor lamb, she trusts you with her babies!"

Mandy nodded. It was a hard thing to do, to take the kitten from her mother, but it was a hard thing Mr. Williams was threatening to do, and Walter's plan made it necessary. "Good girl, Walton," she said. Carefully she folded down the flaps of the cardboard box.

"I hope you know what you're doing!" Mrs. Williams whispered.

Mandy looked her in the face. Her heart was in her mouth as she nodded and went outside. She strapped the box onto her bike, nodded again at Mrs. Williams, tried not to think about Walton and the three cozy kittens in their basket, and set off across the field.

It was the most heart-stopping bike ride she'd ever made. Every bend, every hill she took at snail's pace. She came down into Welford holding her breath. She stopped at the pub, out of sight of Walter and Ernie's row of cottages. Then she unstrapped the box and crept with it in through Walter's open door.

"Got it?" Walter asked.

Mandy nodded. She opened the box. Amy mewed at the light. "Are you sure this will work?" she asked again.

Walter's head went to one side. "Not sure," he said. "Not one hundred percent." He gazed down at tiny, helpless Amy. "She's just a skinny little thing!" He tickled her head.

"Ernie's got a mind of his own. You can bet he'll do exactly the opposite to what you ask. Always has. You say to him, 'Ernie, do me a favor, fix the latch on this back gate for me,' and he'll say straight back, 'What do you think I am, the handyman around here?' and he'll stamp off in the other direction. But if he thinks it's his idea and he sees your gate's broken, he'll make a point of coming up and he'll say, 'I saw your latch needed mending, Walter, so I just got out my toolbox and fixed it for you.' Just like that!"

Mandy understood. "Like rescuing Sammy, you mean? It had to be his idea." She lifted Amy out of her box. "So if he finds a tiny kitten abandoned on his doorstep, he'll take her in?"

Walter nodded. "As long as he does think it's his idea! Then he'll want to keep her and look after her, just like the squirrel. He'll come along to me for advice because he knows I've got the three cats, and I'll suggest, very cunning, how much better it'd be to find a feeding mother until the kitten's properly on its feet. That's where you come in, little miss!"

Mandy looked hard at Amy. "Are you sure?"

He nodded again. "Ernie's got a heart of gold underneath it all!" Walter smiled. "Go on, lass, what have you got to lose? That kitten will have a foster home and be back with her mother before you can say Jack Robinson!"

So Mandy took the precious bundle down the length of the row. Amy squirmed in her hands, mewing piteously. "Shh!" she whispered. Could she do it? Mandy felt as if her heart would stop. Could she leave the poor little thing on a cold doorstep?

She almost stopped to retrace her steps. But what was the alternative? She had less than two days left. Forcing herself to go on, she stooped down by Ernie's front doorstep. She closed her eyes, backed away, and fled down to Walter's house.

"Now we just have to wait," Walter said. They stood inside his doorway, listening to Amy's tiny wail.

"Oh, quick!" Mandy breathed. "Please hear her and come quickly!"

But Ernie's door stayed shut.

Amy mewed her high-pitched sound. Would he hear it? They waited. Mandy leaned forward, desperately wanting to see if Amy was all right. But Walter pulled her back. "You mustn't let him see you!" he warned.

The wait seemed endless. Minutes went by. Amy's tiny howling continued.

Then finally they heard the metal bolts of Ernie's door. They heard the latch turn. The door scraped open. "What the—!" Ernie said. He grunted as he stooped. "Oh-aagh!" They heard him sigh as he picked up the kitten and straightened his old back. He stepped out onto the path. He took time to look up and down. He even carried Amy a few steps towards Walter's house, then he turned and went indoors, carrying the kitten.

"Well?" Mandy was still holding her breath. She looked at Walter.

Walter listened. He considered carefully. Then he brought up one hand in a thumbs-up sign. "I reckon it's worked!" he said.

They had to wait half an hour, maybe more, drinking tea and eating cookies, before they heard Ernie shuffling down the path to Walter's door.

"Say nothing!" Walter warned. "And stay here!"

Mandy nodded.

"Now then, Walter," Ernie said. He poked his head inside the front door. "You know about cats!"

"I do, Ernie," Walter said. "I know something about them, at any rate." Mandy sat out of sight in the kitchen as Walter went down the hall to greet Ernie. "Why, what have you got there?" He managed to sound genuinely surprised.

"Kitten," Ernie said. "What's it look like?" He had wrapped Amy in an old gray sweater. "It's shivering." He showed the little bundle to Walter.

"Yes, it would," Walter said. "It's only a littl'un."

"It just turned up out of the blue," Ernie said. "I was just washing up when I heard it set up a racket on my doorstep! I reckon its mother dropped it there; one too many to look after in the litter!"

"Well, it must be your week for it," Walter said, keeping his voice flat this time. "First the squirrel, now this."

"I dunno about that. It just turned up." Ernie stood there looking helpless. Peeping, Mandy could see the two old men head to head against the square of light in the doorway.

"Ah, well, I reckon you'll have to get rid of this one," Walter said. "Two orphans to look after is more than you can manage."

Mandy gasped and bit her lip. How could he? How could Walter take such a risk?

But Ernie gave Walter his eagle stare. "What do you mean, more than I can manage?" He wrapped Amy up carefully. "I've no intention of getting rid of it, Walter Pickard! No, this little kitten is here to stay!"

Mandy cried. She cried tears of silent joy.

"Aye, but how will you feed it? Look at it, poor little scrap. It needs feeding already," Walter insisted.

Ernie thought about this for a while. "That's why I'm coming to you, Walter. You know about cats."

Now it was Walter's turn to stand there looking awkward and sullen. "It's too young for me to handle. It needs a mother cat," he said. "One that's still feeding her own youngsters."

Ernie squared his shoulders and asked how they would set about finding such a thing; a mother cat that would feed his kitten until it was weaned? He'd like Walter to call the vet right then and there, on his telephone, and get the vet's young girl over there as quick as possible. "I reckon she'll know of just such a cat," Ernie said, hugging Amy to his chest.

"Oh, she'll know," Walter confirmed, giving a little smile.

Back in the kitchen, Mandy grinned. Walter's plan had worked perfectly!

"Then you go ahead and give her a call. You tell her I want her down at my cottage in fifteen minutes sharp!" Ernie instructed. "And tell her to bring something to carry a tiny kitten in. We need a mother cat right away, or my little kitten will starve to death!"

"Right!" Walter agreed.

"Right!" And Ernie marched on back home with Amy.

Walter came back grinning all over his face. Mandy sat on the kitchen stool and smiled through her tears. They'd found a home for Amy. At last they'd found one good home!

Nine

Mandy paid a visit to Ernie's, complete with her lined cardboard box. She fed Amy quickly and expertly, mixing the powdered food in a miniature feeding bottle. She held Amy in one hand, then stroked her abdomen with a forefinger to help her digest the food and get rid of the waste. Ernie didn't bat an eyelid at that.

"You have to do it, otherwise they hang on to it and get constipated," Mandy explained. "That's why the mother cats lick them."

"And how often will this mother cat have to feed it?"

"*She* needs feeding every couple of hours. And the mother will keep her warm, too," Mandy said.

Ernie picked up his kitten and said an awkward goodbye. His fingers looked broad and clumsy against Amy's tiny head, but he held her calmly. He gave her every scrap of his attention. He bent his white head, making encouraging little chucking noises with his tongue. Then he looked up. "I'll call her Tiddles!" he said.

Mandy started to protest, then bit her tongue hard. She couldn't tell Ernie that Amy already had a name. She swallowed and nodded. "Good idea." She took the kitten from Ernie and put her carefully in the box. "She'll be ready to come home in six or seven weeks" she promised.

So Amy became Tiddles. "Brilliant name, isn't it?" She greeted James with the news when they met in the village early next morning. But Mandy was so thrilled that the name hardly mattered. "Three more to go!" she said, full of new enthusiasm for the task. The morning was sunny. Things had begun to go right.

James nodded. He was looking pale and tired.

"What's wrong?" Mandy asked. She was peering in through the post office window to make sure that their card was still up there on the bulletin board.

"Nothing." James shook his head, and started to set off for school. He refused to look Mandy in the face as he mumbled, "Let's go."

"No, there is something wrong!" Mandy insisted. James was always shy and only got visibly excited about football. But today there was something making him even quieter than usual. He hadn't really reacted to the news about Amy. He hadn't said, "Great. Well done. I knew you could do it, Mandy!"

James shook his head again. He was staring down at his sneakers.

Mandy put one hand on the handlebar of his bike. "It's Benji, isn't it?" she said softly.

And James nodded.

"Oh, James, what's wrong with him?" She could have kicked herself. She'd been so full of her own news that she'd forgotten all about poor Benji being ill.

But James couldn't speak. He just sighed.

"He's going to be all right, isn't he? I mean they'll fix him up down at the Ark. It isn't anything serious, is it? What did my mom and dad say?" Mandy was beginning to sense something really awful. She'd never seen James look so sad.

And finally he came out with it. "Benji's dead," he said. "We had to have him put to sleep."

Mandy gasped. She expected the whole sky to come crashing down. Benji was dead. "Why?" She couldn't believe it.

The story came pouring out now. "He had some kind of tumor on his brain. We didn't know it was anything serious, only over the weekend he was a bit groggy. No appetite and so on." James paused to take a deep breath. "He kept staggering. My dad laughed and said he must have been out on Saturday night drinking. He looked pretty sorry for himself, so my mom said we'd take him into the Ark." He paused again and glanced at Mandy. "I think my mom knew," he said.

She nodded. "Then what?" No more Benji, she was thinking. No more Benji curled up on a seat in the Hunters' sunroom. No more Benji leaping from the sloping roof up through the bathroom window. Benji had always been there. He was part of the Hunter family.

James shrugged. He stared hard at his feet again. He was standing astride his bike, head down, miserable. "My mom took him in yesterday. By that time he could hardly stand. It was your mom who looked at him." Mandy realized that nothing in

James's life had ever been so difficult for him to say. "Anyway, she said he had this growth on his brain. And there was nothing to be done in this kind of case."

"So?"

He sniffed. "So your mom explained that he'd be in a lot of pain."

"And *your* mom agreed to have him put to sleep?"

James nodded. "It would have been cruel to let him live."

For a second Mandy's hand touched James's. "That's true," she said.

Then there was a big silence. They both thought of Benji. Patient old Benji who'd grown up with them, who'd always let you pick him up any old way, and who always sat on your lap and let you tickle his chin. He'd put up over the years with all their rough treatment, and he'd never put in a cross word. He was a great cat.

"Let's go!" James said. He glanced around at Mandy. "I told my mom to tell them at the Ark not to say anything to you about it. I wanted to tell you myself."

Mandy nodded and followed on. Life, like the road over to Walton, was full of ups and downs.

It must have been hard for James, she thought, to

help with the kittens this morning. He did the jobs as usual, before school and during lunch break. He listened as Mandy told Mrs. Williams how Amy, alias Tiddles, was safely back with Walton. And her future was secure.

"I hope this Ernie Bell person knows what he's doing with this kitten!" Mrs. Williams said primly. "I mean, men! They don't know how to look after things properly. They're not made that way!"

Mandy raised her eyebrows and glanced at James. He was busy with Smoky's feeding. "Oh, I don't know about that," she said.

"Not my Eric, at least," Mrs. Williams blundered on. "Mind you, he's a bit old-fashioned in that respect."

As if on cue, Mr. Williams tramped in for his lunch. He ate in silence, glancing sullenly at the kitten activity in the far corner of the kitchen. "Tomorrow's D-Day!" he reminded them as he reached for his cap. "And don't you forget!"

D-Day. Death Day. Destruction Day. Deadline Day. Mandy didn't think it was possible to hate someone as much as she hated Mr. Williams just then. He stamped off down the garden path, tweaking a rose bush, perking up a primula.

"He's got to go and see the headmaster!" Mrs.

Williams whispered to Mandy. "He's had the summons!"

Mandy raised her head. She couldn't help that, she thought. And all she really cared about right now was the kitten problem.

"Do you want to go straight home after school?" she asked James, on their way into afternoon classes. She thought there was only so much she could ask him to do, considering Benji.

James looked up at the school shield in the entrance hall. Underneath there was a list of names of men who'd died in two wars, and underneath that was the school motto: "Through Suffering We Succeed!"

"No," he said to Mandy. "I'll be there as usual!"

James must have been thinking about poor Benji all through his games that afternoon. Mandy had glanced out of the science lab window down onto the sports field, and she'd spotted him hanging about miserably on the goal line, most unlike him.

But when they met up after school, his face looked composed, even calm. "I just want to call my mom," he told her. "I'll be there in a minute."

So Mandy went on ahead. As usual, the routine of caring for the kittens took over and she managed to push away the worry about James. She watched with delight their fluffy, wriggling little bodies, their ears beginning to unfold and perk up into position, their bruising battle to feed and to survive.

James came in just as she lifted Eric out of the basket for his feed. She handed the kitten to him. "Here, you feed Eric," she said.

They worked in silence for a few minutes Then James pushed his glasses up the bridge of his nose, sat back, and made an announcement. "I'd like Eric!" He said it quite straightforwardly, just like, "I'd like a candy bar!" or, "Tea with milk but no sugar, please!"

Mandy stared. "What did you say?"

"I'd like Eric," he repeated. "I've thought about it, and I'd like to adopt Eric!"

"Are you sure?" Mandy put Smoky back into the basket. "I mean you're sure it's not too soon after . . . I mean, well, are you *sure?*"

"Yes. I called my mom. She agrees. If we're going to get another cat after Benji, we should do it right away." He looked down, half sad, half happy at the new scrap of life on his lap. "And I'm sure Benji wouldn't mind!"

Mandy waltzed around the kitchen. "Oh, great!" she said. "You hear that, Walton? Oh, brilliant! Oh, James!" She smiled and smiled.

Walton mewed.

There were practical things to arrange. When Mr. Williams threw the kittens out the next day, should James take Eric home then, or could they work out a way to keep Walton and the kittens together until they were weaned? A halfway house. That was the thing to work on, Mandy told James. She looked at Mrs. Williams, who was hovering in the doorway with her·shopping basket.

"Don't ask me!" she muttered darkly. "Eric is in with the headmaster this very minute. Lord knows what's going to happen to any of us!" She went out tightlipped, shaking her head.

"It's something we can work on," Mandy told James as they went out to their bicycles. "A halfway house. Anyway, we have two good homes. Two brilliant homes!" Mandy could have sung for joy as they rode home.

"Two to go!" Mandy told her mom as she flung her schoolbag in the corner of the hallway. She told her about James's decision to take Eric. "He's probably the grumpiest kitten of them all, like the person he's named after," she joked. "But James seems to like him!"

Mrs. Hope smiled. "He's a good boy." Then she

asked Mandy to help in the kitchen. "Your dad's out on an emergency call. One of Mrs. Janeki's sheep. But your grandad called while you were out, just to let us know they're back."

Mandy nodded. "Did they have a good time?"

"He didn't say. But he said your gran had got a reply from the prime minister." Mrs. Hope looked puzzled. "Could that be right?"

"Yes. But that was quick." Mandy asked if she could run up to see them.

"After supper," Mrs. Hope said. She always had to remind her daughter to slow down enough to eat. "What's the point of me preparing all these vegetarian meals for you if you won't even sit down and eat one!" she complained.

Mandy gave her a hug. "Okay, Mom, after supper!"

The camper van sat in the driveway, splashed but splendid. "Hi, Gran! Hi, Grandad!" Mandy burst in on them. She reported the good news about Tiddles ("What a name!") and Eric. She said James was a hero, a real hero!

"Oho!" her grandad raised his eyebrows.

"No, Grandad, not like that!" she said.

"That's what they always say. I think Mandy's got a soft spot for young James."

"Stop teasing, Thomas!" Mandy's gran warned. "Anyway, she's come to see my letter from the Prime Minister, haven't you, love!"

Mandy nodded and laughed. "Sorry, Gran. It's just that the kittens have been taking up all my time. Did you have a good vacation?" she remembered to ask.

There was a small silence. "Yes," Gran said. "But about this letter from 10 Downing Street. See, official notepaper!" She waved the reply in Mandy's face.

"'Yes' means 'Yes, but!,'" Grandad put in. "And then we quickly change the subject!"

"Why, what happened? Did the camper break down?"

"Break down!" he exclaimed. "You must be joking!"

"Of course not," Mrs. Hope said. "The camper was perfect. But Scarborough wasn't."

"Not sunny?"

"Sodden," Mrs. Hope conceded. "Forty-two hours of solid rain. We counted!"

"Ah," Mandy said. "What a shame."

"Yes, but this letter here, see!" Gran waved it before starting to read:

"Dear Mrs. Hope,
The Prime Minister acknowledges receipt of

your letter. While he recognizes your concern about the continued existence of your local sub post office, he wishes me to point out that Government policy on the issue is the concern of one of his junior ministers.

Accordingly he has asked me to pass on this matter to the relevant department.

Yours sincerely,

E. B. Whyte

(Assistant private secretary to

the Prime Minister)"

"There!" Mrs. Hope flung the cream-colored letter onto the table.

"What does it mean?" Mandy asked. "Are they going to close McFarlane's or not?"

"It doesn't mean yes, it doesn't mean no. It doesn't mean anything!" Gran said indignantly.

"It means they've passed the buck," Grandad said. "As usual."

"They won't get away with it!" Gran insisted.

Grandad muttered in a stage whisper, "Watch it, love, she's on the warpath!"

Gran ignored him. "We'll have a campaign. Save our post office!" She stood up and strode across the room.

Mandy was enjoying this, her gran on her high horse.

"I'll have to organize everything, of course!" There was a glint in Gran's eye.

Bells began to ring in Mandy's head. In fact, they set up a giant racket! Did this mean her grandparents would have to put their feet firmly back on Welford ground?

"This'll take a lot of time and energy, Gran," she pointed out.

"Who cares?" Gran swept around the room. "It's important! In fact, it's vital! We'll design a logo for our campaign. A heart shape, to show our post office is at the heart of the village!" Her hair was coming loose from its comb and she was looking very fiery.

"I'm glad I'm not the poor little prime minister!" Grandad laughed.

"Does this mean you might not go to Portugal?" Mandy asked. "I mean, you might have to stay at home more to run this campaign."

Gran stopped in her paces. Grandad said, "Ha!"

"We-ell," Gran said. "We might not go quite so far afield as we thought." She gave Mandy a little grin. "The fact is, we missed you all terribly; you and your mom and dad, and this old place!" She sighed. "We're a pair of old softies, after all!"

"And then there's my tomatoes to consider," Grandad said thoughtfully. "I'll have to talk nicely to my tomatoes!"

Mandy looked at them, bursting to ask the question. She took a great, deep breath. '"Does this mean you might be willing to take a kitten after all?"

They broke into smiles, both of them. They hugged her. "We thought you'd never ask!" They looked at each other. Clearly they'd been thinking about it all the time they'd been away in soggy Scarborough.

"Smoky!" Mandy said, breathless.

"On two conditions," Gran added.

"What?" She glowed with happiness. A home for the third kitten. A home just up the hill from Animal Ark. Mandy couldn't believe it.

"First, you've got to agree to come up and feed him whenever we do go away for a couple of days," Gran said. "When we go off in the camper to lovely Llandudno or wherever."

This was hardly a condition! Mandy nodded, speechless. She'd love to feed Smoky. Then he'd be half hers, wouldn't he! She just sat there nodding.

"Second!" Grandad said, frowning and tryⁱ to look serious. "You must swear to wate tomatoes!"

"Oh, yes," she said. She'd even talk to them. "Oh, yes, yes!"

Ten

Thursday came, and Mandy woke three quarters happy, one quarter sad. Her heart felt pulled apart over Patch; poor little Patch, the only kitten still left homeless.

Mrs. Hope looked at her across the breakfast table. "Problem?" she asked.

"You realize what day it is," Mandy said miserably.

"Thursday," her father said helpfully over the top of his newspaper.

"Yes, Thursday. And I've found homes for three of the kittens in Mr. Williams's kitchen, but there's still one left over! Today's the deadline!" The word "deadline" had an awful hollow ring.

"Hasn't the mother cat decided to move off to a new nest site yet?" Mr. Hope asked.

Mandy shook her head. "No, she's still there in the kitchen, in the laundry basket. And today's the day *he* throws them out!"

"You mean Mr. Williams," Mrs. Hope corrected her. "Not 'he.' So what next?"

"Gran and Grandad say they don't mind if the kittens and Walton move in with them until the kittens are weaned in about six weeks' time." Mandy managed a smile of relief. It had been a close thing all around.

"But?" Mrs. Hope asked.

"But they say the same thing as you. They say I have to find a home for Patch. Otherwise it's cruel to keep him alive!" Her eyes filled. "Poor Patch!"

"It's true. You can't just turn him out to fend for himself when the time comes. He has to have a home!" Even her soft-hearted father was telling her the same thing; the thing she didn't want to hear.

"Dad!" she cried.

"There's no 'Dad!' about it," Mrs. Hope said firmly. "Look, Mandy, you've done brilliantly to find these three homes. We think you're wonderful!"

"Don't!" The tears brimmed over and down her cheeks.

Mrs. Hope looked across at Mr. Hope. Mandy thought she spied a glimmer of hope through her tears. "Listen, love, I'll come over and see you at school this lunchtime, all right?"

"What for?" Mandy said, sniffing and drying her eyes.

"Wait and see. I can't promise anything yet." Mrs. Hope smiled and patted Mandy's hand. "Just wait and see."

That lunchtime Mandy fed Patch with an aching heart. James was busy with little Eric, and the other two kittens were already snuggled down in the basket, when there was a knock at the door.

"Hello. Is Mandy here?" a voice said to Mrs. Williams.

She recognized her mom, but the misery of looking down at Patch's little face, his eyes nearly open now, was too much. She couldn't bear to think about what might have to happen to him.

"Mandy?" her mom's voice repeated.

She looked up.

"I've brought someone with me." Mrs. Hope was gentle but firm, as always. "Come in, and let's have a look at this little fellow."

Mandy felt suddenly surrounded by people and

dragged back to the present from fears of the future. She pulled herself together. "Sorry," she said, standing up with Patch cupped in her hands. Her eyes focused on the visitors: Miss Marjorie and Miss Joan Spry!

What on earth was Mrs. Hope up to? Mandy stood up, ready to protest, but her mom gave her a meaningful look.

"This is the kitten Mandy came to see you about," Mrs. Hope explained calmly. "And I'm sure she apologizes for running off so rudely." She smiled encouragingly at Mandy, who went red and nodded without saying anything.

The two sisters nodded back and peered down at Patch. They poked their thin faces towards him curiously. They looked silently at each other.

Mandy had gotten over her shock. She trusted her mom to know what she was doing. And today the Spry twins didn't look so strange. Their untidy hair was combed back underneath straw hats, and their pastel summer coats made them look like quaint wedding guests.

"This is the only kitten left without a home," Mandy said. She offered Patch to one of the twins, not knowing which one.

The twin shook her head. "No, give him to Joan.

See if she likes him," Miss Marjorie said. "She did promise to try and like him!"

Mandy held out the kitten again. With shaking hands Miss Joan took the little fur scrap and cradled it. She brought her face close to the kitten's and felt it lick her finger. "What is its name?" she breathed.

"Patch," Mandy said, holding her own breath. "He's just one week old!"

Joan looked up at her sister. The silence held them all like a net. Would she say yes? Would she give Patch a home and a future?

"Yes," she said at last. "I think I like him!"

"Of course you do! What did I tell you!" Miss Marjorie said.

And they all smiled and congratulated one another. They listened to Mandy's instructions about how a kitten should be treated: "Don't poke him, don't press him too hard, don't disturb him too much!" She said they should put him back with his mother now. "The excitement's too much for him," she said as she returned a squeaking Patch to his warm, dark nest.

The Spry twins smiled and thanked Mandy and went off happily through the porch, arm in arm.

"See!" Mrs. Hope said, head to one side. "Didn't I say they were harmless? You have to learn that all people are different, but that doesn't make them wrong. This kitten will be the best thing that's happened to the twins in an awfully long time!"

Mandy laughed and hugged her mom. "Oh, thanks!" she said. A great weight had lifted off her chest. She sighed and looked in on the kittens. They were curled up, snug and warm against Walton's sleeping body. "Four homes! We did it!"

"You did it," Mrs. Hope said. "You and James!"

They looked at each other with huge grins on their faces. James went red, even before Mandy hugged him.

When Miss Marjorie came back in for a moment, James leaped back. Dainty as a canary in her pale yellow coat, she made straight for Mandy. "Thank you, my dear!" she said, patting her hand. "Thank you for bringing life back into our dark, dreary house. It's all due to you!" She beamed, nodded lightly at James. "I'd best get back to my sister. We'll wait for you in the car," she told Mrs. Hope before walking off again.

"Happy now?" Mandy's mom asked.

Her eyes shone with tears again. She nodded and they nearly spilled over. This time Mandy could say nothing at all!

* * *

School ended and the great move began. "It's time for a new nest, Walton," Mandy told her gently. "And you don't even have to do it yourself, you lucky cat!"

"You're sure it'll be all right now?" Mrs. Williams fussed. There was no sign of her husband. It was a heavy day, threatening rain when Mandy's grandparents' camper van pulled up in the playground. "Walton won't desert these kittens now?" She stood at the kitchen sink, grasping a tea towel.

"No, it'll work out okay, Mrs. Williams. Don't worry!" Mandy looked up and realized the old lady would miss Walton and the kittens after all. She smiled. "Honestly, Walton would fight to the death for them now. She's made a good strong bond with them. Thanks to you, of course!"

"Oh!" Mrs. Williams raised her hands and smiled modestly.

"Yes, you gave them a good start. Now my gran and grandad will keep a close eye on them up at Lilac Cottage!"

"Then what?" Mrs. Williams folded her tea towel into a precise rectangle. She laid it down on the drain board and smoothed it carefully.

"Then James will take Eric and give him a home," Mandy said, handing the kitten to him.

"And me and my wife will keep this little chap," Grandad said, lifting Smoky in one hand.

"Ernie Bell is waiting to have Amy—er—Tiddles. And now Patch has found a home at The Riddings!" Mandy counted them off on her fingers.

Mrs. Williams sniffed and nodded. "And what about Walton?"

Mandy looked at James. "We haven't got that far!"

He shrugged. "We have a bit of time to sort it out."

"Well, I'll have to have a word with my Eric," Mrs. Williams said. But she would say no more.

So they drove off in triumph in the silver camper; cat and kittens, James, Mandy, and her grandad.

Walton quickly regained her strength in the sunny warmth of Lilac Cottage. After three more weeks Smoky, Patch, Tiddles, and Eric began to bounce and tumble. They chased anything that moved. On Mr. Hope's lawn they sat in wait for butterflies to land on the purple buddleia. Still as statues, they watched and waited. Then they bounced and pounced and tumbled. They always missed. They turned endless somersaults. Mandy would score them out of ten like international gymnasts doing their floor exercises.

James came often to check on Eric. He lay propped

on his elbows out on the lawn, with a computer magazine spread out in front of him. He pretended to read, but really he watched Eric's every move; his grumpy swipes with his front paws at mischievous Smoky and Patch, his sulking under the shade of the rhubarb leaves.

"Don't worry," Mandy said. "After a week in your house he'll be as sweet-tempered and patient as poor old Benji was. It's the Hunters' magic way with cats!"

James looked up from his magazine and smiled.

Mandy went down regularly to the village to report to Ernie on Tiddles's progress. Ernie would ask endless questions about his kitten and waited with utter impatience for the day when he could have her home. "Hey!" he warned Sammy, flipping the squirrel off his shoulder. "Stop nipping my ear, you!" The squirrel, who had free range of Ernie's kitchen, scampered down his back and around his waist, to cling on to his belt buckle.

Mandy laughed. "He'll be jealous when Tiddles comes!"

"And so he should be," Ernie said. "I can't wait to get that kitten home!"

At Lilac Cottage, Walton fed the four kittens less and less, watched them take to solid food and grew rather bored with motherhood. These days she preferred a quiet corner in the kitchen underneath the vegetable rack, with a bit of peace and quiet. Her job was almost done.

Mid-term vacation arrived. It was a green world; everyone was packing up and going home.

"Now, then," Mr. Williams grunted at Mandy by way of greeting. She was unlocking the padlock on her bike.

She glanced up. It was unusual for the custodian to talk to her at all these days, and it was weeks since she'd seen his wife. "Oh, great!" she muttered.

She hadn't forgiven him for hanging that dreadful

threat over their heads, even though things had worked out fine in the end. The best she could do was to avoid the custodian whenever possible. She hastily got ready to push off for home.

"How are those kittens of yours?" Mr. Williams grumbled in his low, gravelly voice. "Getting pretty big and strong by now, I should think?"

Mandy nodded.

"And I hear you've found folk willing to take them on?" he persisted. One hand was on his precious garden gate, but he looked like a man with something on his mind.

Oh, go away, just go away! Mandy thought to herself.

But instead he said, "Come here a second," and looked around furtively at the lace curtains of the kitchen window. "I want to have a word!"

It involved Mandy riding back to school on the first day of her mid-term vacation. She had the basket strapped carefully to the back of her bike. *Who would have believed it?* she thought to herself as she lifted the basket, reached in, and gathered Walton gently in her arms.

"Come on, Walton, come on, girl!" she murmured.

"Shh!" said Mr. Williams, gesturing towards the porch. "This is still a secret!"

Mandy nodded and set Walton down. Immaculate, ladylike, and elegant as a model on a catwalk, Walton sniffed the logs, tested the doormat, pushed the door with her paw. It swung open.

"Eric?" Mrs. Williams called from inside the kitchen. Mandy grinned at the custodian. Then, "Eric!" Mrs. Williams said again, her voice high-pitched and surprised. "Eric, this cat has just walked back into this kitchen as if she owns the place!"

They went inside to see, and there was Mrs. Williams staring down at the familiar black and white shape. "How did she get here? Did she walk?" Mrs. Williams demanded.

Her husband gave a self-conscious little laugh. "No, as a matter of fact, Amy, I asked this young lady here to bring her back home for you!"

Mrs. Williams looked up at him, her eyes filling with tears. "Oh, Eric!"

"Yes, well!" He looked embarrassed. "I knew you were pining for the darn cat." He half turned towards Mandy. "She pestered me to death about it! She's too soft by half, my wife!'

Mandy watched Walton wrap herself around Mrs. Williams's legs, purring like mad. She peered in her corner for food and looked up as if to say, "Where is it, then?" They laughed, gave her a saucer of milk and made a great fuss of her homecoming.

"And will we take her with us?" Mrs. Williams asked, still unable to believe her husband's change of heart.

"Why, where are you going?" Mandy asked.

"Eric's leaving his job."

"He's not. . .?" Mandy looked anxiously at the old couple. Had Mr. Williams's arthritis finally beaten him?

"No, he hasn't been fired," Mrs. Williams said. "No, in fact the headmaster only wanted to see him to ask him to stay on beyond retirement age. He said he'd never find another custodian as good as Eric!"

Mr. Williams tut-tutted.

"Yes, he did, Eric! But he came home and we talked about it, and we decided of our own accord that we'd call it a day. We're getting on a bit and we want some peace and quiet in our old age."

Mr. Williams nodded. He watched Walton grooming herself after her drink. She was sitting on the windowsill, using her front paw to clean behind her ears. "Well!" he said, taken aback.

"I told you they're nice clean animals!" Mandy laughed.

"So we've decided to retire!" Mrs. Williams announced. "We've got our eye on one of the new bungalows just up the road!"

"A quiet little cul-de-sac, plenty of garden!" Mr. Williams said.

"Perfect for Walton?" Mandy could hardly keep the smile from spreading all over her face.

The custodian looked at his wife and broke into a grin. "I suppose so," he said, shaking his head.

"And will it be all right if I book Walton in at Animal Ark for her operation?" Mandy asked, trying to be tactful.

"Operation?" Mr. Williams repeated slowly.

"Yes, so she won't have any more kittens."

"Oh," he said, very old-fashioned. "*That* operation!"

"Yes, you don't want any more little ones cluttering up your kitchen, getting in among your best shirts!"

Mr. Williams went bright red. He looked sheepishly at his wife, then his face broke into a broad grin again. "I should say not!" he agreed.

So Mandy made the arrangements. She wouldn't hear of them having to pay for Walton being spayed. She knew her mom and dad would want that too. So she said she would book Walton in for the following Monday. Mandy took the hand offered by Mr. Williams and shook it warmly.

"No hard feelings?" he asked.

"None!" she said.

* * *

Mandy rode home along the field road. She felt on top of the world, literally. The road crested the hill. Lapwings curved overhead in the clear sky, the fields rolled in every direction. Perfect!

She headed downhill to Welford and Animal Ark. She'd go in to see who else needed rescuing; maybe a lost hedgehog who'd found its way to the exam room, or a "male" hamster who'd just produced six babies! ("The pet shop said it was a boy, they did really!")

The wind caught Mandy's hair. She tilted her head back and stuck her legs out sideways to freewheel down the hill. And she laughed out loud.